MW01129104

THE
GIFT

A MAGERI SERIES NOVELLA

USA TODAY BESTSELLING AUTHOR
DANNIKA DARK

Also By Dannika Dark:

THE MAGERI SERIES
Sterling
Twist
Impulse
Gravity
Shine
The Gift (Novella)

NOVELLAS
Closer

THE SEVEN SERIES
Seven Years
Six Months
Five Weeks
Four Days
Three Hours
Two Minutes
One Second
Winter Moon (Novella)

SEVEN WORLD
Charming

Dear Reader

SPOILER WARNING: If you have not read the Mageri series, this book will make no sense. I wanted to give Mageri fans another glimpse of their favorite characters. The story takes place *after* the Mageri series (including *Risk*). Please begin with *Sterling*, the first book in the Mageri series.

The journey is worth it.

To my loyal Mageri readers: This stocking stuffer was written and wrapped with love. Thank you for allowing these characters to live on in your hearts.

CHAPTER 1

Silver and Logan

LOGAN APPROACHED ME FROM BEHIND and placed his hands on my shoulders. "Silver, do you want to talk about it?"

I shook my head, crestfallen. It was the second time that year that we'd lost a child to nefarious buyers on the black market. Logan and I weren't able to conceive children of our own; nature had no intention of bending the rules for a Chitah and a Mage. The orphanage had turned us away, so we'd resorted to bidding for children on the black market.

Logan Cross made me happier than any woman could dream, and I was blessed to have him as my kindred spirit. I sometimes thought back to when we first met—when I was so lost in this unimaginable new world. This dark and mysterious man who had been hired to kidnap me ended up saving my life in more ways than one. Even after years of living together, I still got butterflies when he looked at me with those beautiful amber eyes. Logan was a doting, protective lover who carried

8 DANNIKA DARK

me to bed whenever I fell asleep watching TV. He cooked most of our meals, threatened any man who disrespected me, and always kept my feet warm on winter nights.

We lived in a private building with Logan's brothers and my Ghuardian, Justus, though they resided on separate floors. I still received Mage training from Justus, and I was surrounded by people I considered my family. Life couldn't be more perfect.

Except for that one thing I couldn't give Logan.

The one thing he said didn't matter.

But it did.

Even though I couldn't have children, it didn't negate my desire to share the experience of parenting with him. Fate might have removed one option, but Logan was determined to pursue another. He was born to be a father. Not only was it in his DNA, but he had so much love to give—so much to teach. I wanted to see him hold a baby in his arms while it grabbed fistfuls of his blond hair, and I wanted to feel the joy of watching our child grow. I'd never dared to dream so big, but Logan made anything seem possible.

"Female, I can scent your pain."

I gazed out the window at the snowfall blanketing the dark city, ignoring Logan's reflection in the glass. "That's the second time this year one slipped through our fingers. It's hard enough not getting a child for my own selfish purposes, but it's even worse to think how we failed at saving those children. God knows where they are now or who bought them."

He rested his chin on my head. "We can only hope there are others like us who are searching for the same reasons—who are willing to pay anything for such a privilege."

"I hope so," I whispered.

Logan wrapped his strong arms around me, and I drew in his masculine smell. "Trust in the fates, Little Raven. Don't let our failures destroy us. I'm not going anywhere."

I turned around and nestled against his chest. "I know. I just didn't think it would be this hard. Now I'm depressed all over again, and it's almost Christmas. You might as well just leave me here and go celebrate with everyone else."

He rocked with laughter. "I'm hardly leaving my female alone during a festive occasion. It's not like you to sulk."

I peered up at him. "You're not the one who's going to be cooking for seventeen people. And half of them are men who can single-handedly put an all-you-can-eat buffet out of business."

He furrowed his sexy brow. Logan's face had the characteristics of a predator: a broad nose at the bridge, a heavy brow, a terrifying gaze, and a wide smile. "Sounds like someone's getting her usual holiday jitters. Why should something as innocuous as dinner make you nervous? We're family."

I stepped back. "Because! I have to make sure there's enough food, time everything, do all the dishes—"

"Alone?" he asked, shifting his stance. Strands of long blond hair obscured one eye when he tilted his head to the side.

I'd insisted on doing Christmas dinner myself since in the past Sunny and Page had always volunteered to cook on special occasions. The least I could do was give them one holiday where they could enjoy their children and not have to slave over a hot stove.

"There'll be plenty of food," Logan assured me, swaggering toward the kitchen.

"Oh really? Because last I checked, one oven isn't enough to feed the Cross family." I glanced in the mirror and saw my dark hair was all scrambled up, so I reached in my pocket and retrieved a hair tie. "I'm getting up early since I'll be cooking all day tomorrow. The more I can get done in advance, the better. My plan is to knock out the desserts since they'll keep for a few days anyhow. Then tomorrow night, I'll prepare some of the side dishes. Obviously not the dressing or hot foods, except for beans. I have a slow cooker to keep those warm. Levi likes potato salad, and I'm making those homemade yeast rolls that Finn's always begging for. We're having turkey and ham. Hopefully that's enough meat for everyone."

Logan stood barefoot, peering into the fridge. He finally decided on a bag of cheese cubes and turned around, walking me backward. "We can cater. No one will know."

"I'll know."

He kept advancing until my back was to the wall. "Why must you do this alone? I offered to help."

"You don't help; you take over."

His eyes were brimming with concern. "You won't enjoy the day if you're exhausted. I don't like seeing my female stressed and overworked."

"I need this distraction," I admitted.

He didn't need me to describe the pain that was squeezing my chest, an ache that always appeared during the holidays. Logan owned a map of my heart, and he knew every fracture, every river, and every canyon.

He bent down and planted a chaste kiss on my mouth. When a purr rumbled deep in his chest, I sank into his embrace. Damn, I loved it when that man purred. Sometimes late at night when he thought I was asleep, he'd pull me tight against him and turn on his motor. There was nothing sexier. Logan Cross was six and a half feet of pure male, and he was all mine.

I gazed up at his golden eyes rimmed in black and touched his long hair. "Mr. Cross?"

He tilted his head to the side. "Yes?"

"Hand over the cheese. That's not for snacking on until Christmas."

He inclined his head and smiled fiendishly. "As you wish, my sweet. But only on one condition."

"Oh? And what's that?"

Logan wrapped his arm around my waist and lifted me onto the counter. He wedged himself between my legs and nuzzled against my neck, sending goose pimples across my skin. The bag of cheese fell to the floor as he sensually brushed his lips along my jaw, making me blush with desire. "You may belong to the kitchen tomorrow, but tonight you're *mine*."

CHAPTER 2

Silver and Logan

E VERYONE IN OUR SIX-STORY RESIDENCE had their own floor except for Sadie and Leo. When Sadie first met up with her brothers, she wanted to get to know them, so living with Leo wasn't a bad situation. But after a while they both needed their own space. Justus was working with a builder to add an additional level for Sadie, but it was going to take time.

Lucian lived on the first floor where the family room, gym, and study were located. He preferred less square footage, so his apartment only took up a small space on the west side. Since he was a computer whiz and did contract work, Lucian pulled his weight monitoring our security systems, fingerprint scanners, and the underground parking garage. Someone had to watch the cameras for trespassers and make sure the equipment was working properly, and it gave Justus more time to focus on his cases and raise a family.

Finn lived on the second floor, Justus and Page above him,

then Levi on the fourth, Logan and I on the fifth, and finally Leo and Sadie on the top floor. We had two levels of underground parking, and I often teased Justus that we could just convert one of those into living quarters. But Justus wasn't about to give up real estate meant for his growing car collection. Aside from family, Justus had one passion in life: expensive vehicles.

Justus still retained his status as my Ghuardian, and even though he no longer had any say in making decisions for me, he acted as my advisor and made sure my physical Mage training was up to par. Between that and working as an apprentice for Novis, I had my hands full. Even though my Mage powers surpassed almost everyone else's, careers weren't handed out on a silver platter. You had to put in your time, work hard, and build your reputation.

And there was so much to learn in our world.

I put another apple pie in the oven and set the timer. Logan and I had spent the previous night naked in bed. He usually slept in the nude, but last night we were doing anything but sleeping. Just remembering the feel of his mouth on my bare thigh made me lose my concentration.

"Something smells good," he purred from behind me. "And it's not the pie."

"Quit sniffing my emotions." I slapped him playfully with a kitchen towel covered in flour. "Can you run down to Levi's and bring the cakes up here? Something tells me he's going to try to slice off an end and re-ice it. If he eats all the desserts, he's going to have to deal with Justus."

"Why Justus?"

"Because Rose loves sweets, and her tears are his kryptonite."

Logan chuckled. "I've already issued Levi a warning that if he puts one finger on my female's cake, his residency here will be terminated."

I turned around, the red oven mitt still on my hand. "You wouldn't really do that, would you?"

He stepped forward, his gaze piercing mine. "I've never made an empty threat. Brother or not, no man touches my female's lemon cake."

Typical Logan.

"Well, let's avoid a family feud and bring them up to remove all temptation. You guys can carry everything down tomorrow morning. I think Page bought special tablecloths, so don't put anything on the table until those are down. We need someone to get all the dishes, wine, condiments, silverware—"

Logan pressed his finger against my lips. "Everything's taken care of. You won't have to lift a finger, and Little Wolf volunteered to decorate the room."

I arched my eyebrows. "Finn?"

"He's shopping with Lucian."

"That should be interesting."

Lucian was the quieter Cross brother. He was the only one with black hair, a rare and undesired trait among Chitahs.

Lucian was an intellectual and more introverted than his gregarious brothers. Because of his insomnia, he was usually up at odd hours doing programming work. Between his dark hair and five-ten stature, strangers treated him differently when they found out he was a Chitah. Perhaps that's why he got along with Finn so well. Even though Finn was a Shifter, those two had a lot in common when it came to the adversities they faced in our world.

I tossed the oven mitt on the counter and stared at Logan's red sneakers. "What about Justus?"

Logan lifted my chin with the crook of his finger. "He and Simon are out buying a tree."

I sputtered with laughter. "Whose idea was that? These are men who don't do Christmas. Simon's liable to put panties and handcuffs on the tree, and Justus will probably buy the smallest one they have just to get out of there."

Logan lifted a box that contained icing, colorful sprinkles, and powdered sugar. "I'll take these down to Levi's and ice everything myself."

"But—"

"Don't argue or I'll ice *you* instead," he growled sexily.

I wasn't sure whether to let him go or put up a fight. If disobedience meant him licking icing off my body, then maybe I needed to go on the naughty-girl list.

CHAPTER 3

Justus and Simon

J USTUS'S NECK FLUSHED WITH EMBARRASSMENT the moment he entered the human establishment. Humans he had no problem with. It was the garish display of tinsel and twinkling lights that offended him. He beheld the Christmas decorations that stretched in every direction and shuddered at the holiday music blaring across the loudspeakers. Music was meant to be a gift to the senses, not an assault.

Justus was a simple man, and Page shared the same taste when it came to decorating their home on the holidays. She usually set a few candles on the windowsill and mantel. When the mistletoe made an appearance, Justus insisted on putting a sprig in every doorway. That was one tradition he was determined to keep.

Sometimes they decorated the family room with a few candles and a strand or two of lights, but they had never done anything this elaborate.

This was the first year since moving into the building that

everyone was going to be home for Christmas. Last year, Justus had been out of the state on assignment. Leo had gone with him since they both worked for HALO. When everyone's schedules aligned this year, Silver insisted on cooking dinner and spending the whole day together. Justus had a good laugh about that. Silver was inept in the kitchen and didn't work well under stress. Why she'd volunteered for such an undertaking was beyond his understanding, but Page was surreptitiously helping out on the side. She planned on making fruit and vegetable platters to snack on since none were listed on the menu posted in the family room downstairs.

Simon waved. "Oi! Justus, this looks like a winner." His British accent and leathers were causing a stir among the female shoppers.

Simon strutted across the platform, comparing his height to a nine-foot silver tree.

"Not that one," Justus grumbled.

"Why the bloody hell not? Seems fitting considering our hostess is named Silver." Simon laughed like a hyena and jumped onto the next platform, his boots stomping on the wood.

"Sir, get down from there," a woman snapped from the customer-service counter. Her lips were so tightly pressed together that the skin around her mouth was whiter than the rest of her face.

Some of the Christmas trees were on platforms that

stretched down the center aisle toward the back of the store. To the left and right were rows upon rows of ornaments, lights, and inflatable monstrosities. Justus shook his head. This place looked like a warehouse where tinsel went to die. His ancestors would roll over in their graves if they knew they'd died nobly on battlefields so that their descendants could buy things like pink trees and singing snowmen.

Justus felt the urge to bolt when a woman strutted by him wearing a green sweater sporting a reindeer with a red blinking nose.

He stalked forward and pointed at a tree. "That one."

Simon jumped down to the floor, in leather from neck to heel, and adjusted himself as he stared up at the black tree. "That's a bit morbid. Shall we look for a grim reaper to put on top? I'll ask the lady if she has a death shroud to wrap around as garland. Maybe we can find some miniature sickle ornaments."

Justus was dressed down in a pair of jeans and a skintight black shirt. He'd left the house in a hurry and had forgotten his jacket. Thermals didn't need to worry about keeping warm, but he usually dressed appropriately for the weather, especially around humans.

Simon stopped and jerked his head toward the right. "How about this one?"

Justus swung his gaze up at the pink tree and then gave Simon a frosty glare.

His outspoken friend arched an eyebrow, and his tousled

hair slipped in front of his eyes. "I can see your nipples through your shirt. In another hour, you're going to look like the Pied Piper with a harem following you. Maybe we should hurry this along."

After a short walk, they stopped in front of a large green tree with built-in white lights. Without a word, they nodded at each other and it was decided.

Simon clapped his hands together, his fingerless gloves muffling the sound. "Now for the dressing. Let's have some fun, shall we?" He grabbed a green cart someone had parked at the end of an aisle.

Justus glared at a wall of colorful plastic ornaments. He turned one in his hand. "Why would these humans put a sumo wrestler on their tree?"

Simon held a hook between two fingers. "I found a pickle." He tossed it into the basket. "Bloody hell, look at *this*!" Two ornaments crashed onto the floor when he yanked one out by the string. "This one has your name all over it."

Justus tried to feign indifference as he stared at the Mercedes. "That one's acceptable."

Simon placed his foot on the undercarriage of the cart and leaned over the front so he could ride it down the aisle.

Hundreds of years later and Simon hadn't changed a bit.

Justus found an ornament shaped like the state of Texas, where Silver was from. After checking out a few more aisles, Simon picked out a Rubenesque woman for Justus, a pair of red sneakers for Logan, and a wolf for Finn. Justus added a few more cars, a crocheted star for Page, and a little rose for his Rose.

An hour later, they had filled two shopping carts.

"Think we've gone overboard?" Simon asked, arms folded as he examined their wares. "A lady three aisles over said we have to buy a skirt for the tree. Maybe you can borrow one from Page's wardrobe. She also mentioned stockings. Does Page wear garters?"

"One more word and I'll throttle you. And remove that hat before I set it on fire."

Simon pursed his lips, his musical Santa hat moving left to right, bells jingling on the fluffy white ball. "Bah, humbug! There was a whole aisle on Scrooge. Be right back while I pick out *your* ornaments." He swaggered off, removing his leather coat and tossing it over his shoulder like some kind of fashion model from a BDSM club.

Justus rubbed his chin, wondering if they'd gotten everything.

"You look a little lost. Is there something you're looking for?"

He turned to face a beautiful blonde with bright red lips and an eager smile. "Are you employed here?"

Her breasts jiggled when she laughed. "No, I just couldn't help but notice your defeated expression. I come here every year, so I know these aisles like the back of my hand."

This human was succumbing to his Charmer gift. Sexual energy melted off him like warm chocolate, and it usually attracted any woman standing within a few feet. He'd been doing his best to distance himself from the crowd, but every so often, he'd turn a corner and women would start undressing him with their eyes.

Justus cleared his throat and stepped back. "I'm here with a friend. We're shopping for our... wives," he said, hoping to discourage her.

A loud crash sounded from a nearby aisle. Everyone briefly turned to look before going about their business.

The blonde batted her long lashes. "Too bad. Looks like they're missing out on all the fun. Are you sure that—"

"I'm positive," he said, holding up his hand. "We prefer to be alone."

Hopes dashed, she turned away slowly. Justus gave her a cold, impassive stare, hoping it would be enough to drive her away. The last thing he wanted was to hurt a woman's feelings, but leading her on was cruel when he had all the woman he could ever want waiting for him at home.

His head was pounding to the beat of the loudspeaker music, so he took a seat next to an inflatable snowman. Two kids shrieked and sprinted by, one chasing the other with a giant candy cane.

Seconds later, Simon flashed to his side.

Justus lurched to his feet, his lips peeled back. "You can't do that in here! They have security cameras."

Simon scratched the back of his neck. "I think we need to go. I broke something expensive."

CHAPTER 4

Page and Rose

P AGE FINISHED SLICING THE LAST of the carrots and put them in plastic bags to keep them from drying out. She polished the trays in preparation for the morning. Tomorrow was Christmas Day, and they were going to spend it together from dawn until dusk. No television, computers, or other electronics. Only good food, board games, conversation, music, and family.

Page felt guilty about Silver doing most of the work, but she also knew that it would be something Silver could look back on proudly. The Cross men were Chitahs, and by nature they didn't believe a woman's place was in the kitchen or serving men. It was a miracle Silver had convinced them to let her do this alone, but she was a headstrong woman who loved proving herself.

Page and Sunny knew from experience that cooking for these men was an undertaking, and since it was going to be an all-day event, they'd secretly decided to bring chips, dips, and snacks for between meals. Meanwhile, Leo and Levi were shoveling snow to clear the walkways outside the building in case anyone wanted to go for a walk.

Page strode into the living room and caught her reflection in the floor mirror. She approached the glass and touched the ends of her brown hair, which she kept above her shoulders in a tapered cut. Short or not, it looked a mess after all the work she'd been doing. Her hand traveled down to her stomach, which wasn't flat. Despite all the training after pregnancy, she'd never regained her old figure.

How could Justus, a man who could have any woman he wanted and who'd always had such high standards about everything in his life, find her so beautiful? Maybe his reverent words and unwavering love were why she'd never had the desire to change. She worked out to stay fit and healthy, but that was the extent of it. Page didn't bother with heels to appear taller, nor had she grown out lustrous locks of hair. She was a Relic, and her body aged and changed like a human's. Yet that made no difference to the immortal she shared her bed with.

"Mommy! It won't go on."

Rose stood before her with tears glittering in her eyes. A red barrette was hanging askew in her blond hair.

Page knelt down and removed the bow, which had strands of her hair tangled around it. She smoothed out Rose's hair and then placed the clip above her ear. "There you go, sweetie."

Rose touched her barrette and glanced in the mirror. "Acceptable," she said, a miniature version of her father.

Page chuckled and straightened Rose's red velvet dress. The top half was black with short sleeves, and a bow around her waist accented the red skirt. It was supposed to be her special outfit for tomorrow, but Rose wanted to wear it both days, and Page had agreed. Why not? Rose was going to be four soon and would never be three again. It seemed like just yesterday that she was a baby. Page remembered fondly how she'd sometimes wake up to find Justus sleeping in the nursery by the crib.

Rose mirrored her father in some ways and Page in others. She had Page's big brown eyes, Justus's natural blond hair, and a dash of her own uniqueness. Despite Justus spoiling her to no end, Rose had a tender heart and caring soul. She was intelligent, well-spoken for her age, and fascinated by elderly people. Sometimes in public she'd approach them and ask questions. Immortals didn't grow old, and those Breeds who lived an extended lifespan aged slowly. Rose seemed to grasp these details and had become interested in the aging process.

"Mommy, can I have just one peppermint?"

Page shook her head. "Let's save the treats for tomorrow. It'll give you something to look forward to. Tonight your daddy's going to read you some new stories."

Rose smiled brightly and dashed into the hallway. "I'm going to watch it snow in the playroom!"

"If you want to go outside later, you'll have to change out of that dress."

Page gazed toward the expansive living room windows.

Time flew by so quickly. Eventually Rose would stop aging and take on the immortal traits of a Mage. No one else like Rose existed. Page couldn't explain how she knew the things she did about her daughter; that insight was acquired during pregnancy. Rose would not only inherit the knowledge on her Relic side, but she would also one day have the full power of a Mage. With each passing year her core light grew stronger, and because she was also a Creator, it meant that even though she wouldn't be able to have children, she could have progeny to pass down her legacy.

A knock sounded at the door, stealing Page away from her thoughts.

On her way to answer, she grabbed a brown sweater jacket from a hook and put it on.

When she opened the door, Levi greeted her with a sheepish grin. "Hey, mind if I hang out here for a while? Logan booted me out so he can ice cakes."

Page cast a critical eye at Levi, known for his hearty appetite. "Do you like raw vegetables?"

He wrinkled his nose.

"Come on in."

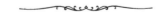

Hours later, Levi had fallen asleep on her sofa after talking her ears off about something he saw on the Discovery channel. She covered him with a thin blanket and took the bag of sourdough pretzels out of his hand. When his snoring grew louder, Rose giggled from a nearby room.

Their living room had floor-to-ceiling windows overlooking the west side of Cognito. The couch faced the right wall where the television was, something they didn't turn on very often except for when Rose wanted to watch cartoons.

Page hugged her arms, watching the snow blanketing the city. They lived in a private Breed district that had once been a location for factories and warehouses, so they didn't have the nuisance of traffic on their street. Being on the third floor didn't give them the best view, but they also didn't have any tall buildings in the way.

Justus hadn't responded to her last text message. He often ignored the phone while driving so he wouldn't cause an accident. Page couldn't help but worry. He could still die if the car caught fire, and after having been in a car accident herself recently, the thought of him trapped beneath two tons of crushing steel terrified her. Life didn't come with guarantees. His being immortal didn't stop her from worrying about his safety. Justus was her world, and life would stop without him.

She turned her back to the window and looked around. Their living room was an open space with grey couches and basic furniture. Straight ahead was the front door, and to the left was the kitchen in a separate room. Since the elevators were in the center of the building, the house wrapped around like a square donut. To the right was the study, and down the hall was

Rose's room, a bathroom, Justus's office, Page's office, a family library, and then their bedroom in the back corner. Left along the back of the house was Rose's playroom, another bathroom, two spare rooms, and then a sunroom on the northeast corner that ran along the left side of the house. Justus had built a door that connected it to the kitchen so they wouldn't have to walk around the entire house to get to the front door. For safety reasons, he didn't want multiple entryways into the apartment.

That was Justus. Always thinking about ways to protect them. They even had fire sprinklers installed and a trap door for emergencies.

A beep sounded at the door from the thumbprint scanner and Page turned around, her heart quickening.

When Justus sauntered in, he still had snow on his hat.

Page blew out a breath and hurried toward him, her arms wide. "I was worried about you."

The moment his lips met with hers, he turned on his internal heater, melting away her worries. Justus tasted divine, and she kissed him harder. He encircled her waist with his strong arms and growled approvingly when her tongue met his. If Justus was anything, he was a masterful kisser. He had a way of making every kiss feel like the first time.

They broke the kiss when a bright giggle erupted from below.

Rose smiled up at Justus. "Like my dress, Daddy?"

He stepped back, his brows drawn together as he gazed

down at his little girl. "She looks too grown-up. She's just a baby."

"I'm not a baby," Rose said, her smile waning.

Page warned him with a glare that he better compliment Rose's dress or else he was going to have to deal with waterworks.

Justus knelt down and kissed Rose on the forehead. "*Très jolis*. My little girl is growing up too fast."

Rose wrapped her arms around his neck. "Nuh-uh. I'm still little. You can pick me up."

Justus scooped her up with one arm and stood. Then he placed quick kisses on her neck until his whiskers made her giggle and squirm. He hadn't always been an affectionate man, and he still struggled with it in public, but when it came to Page and Rose, they were the exceptions to the rule. Justus never withheld his affection from either of them, especially Rose.

He said something to her in French.

Rose nodded. "*Oui.*"

"*Très bien, mon petit ange.*" He winked at Page, and while she had no idea what he had said, *mon ange* was a term of endearment that he'd given Page a long time ago. Sometimes he called Rose his little angel.

He set her down, and she took off toward the front door while Justus gave Page another long and thoughtful kiss. She felt protected in his arms, as if he could shield her from all the dangers in the world. Justus was six feet tall with broad shoulders, tattoos on his right arm and back, a warrior's gaze, and closely shaven hair. He wasn't the kind of man she had ever imagined herself falling for, but he was noble, loving, and a gifted artist.

Unfortunately, he had given up painting centuries ago, so Page had recently converted one of their spare rooms into a studio. It didn't seem right to let his talent go to waste, and he spent so much time working on cases that it seemed like a good way to help him relax. She bought canvases, paint, and brushes in hopes that it would awaken the passion he'd long given up. He hadn't brought the subject up, but it warmed her heart each time she spied him sneaking into the room.

"Wow!" Rose shrieked from the hall.

Curious, Page moved around Justus and peered outside. There were bags upon bags of Christmas ornaments and tinsel spilling onto the floor.

"Why didn't you leave everything downstairs?"

His neck turned red. "I didn't want anyone to see. It took me three trips to get it all up here."

She laughed. "Well, you're just going to have to face the hecklers and take it all back down. You're the one on tree duty, and that means *you* decorate. Hiding the evidence isn't going to make it go away."

His shoulders sagged.

Page furrowed her brow as Rose opened a bag and revealed how many items were inside. "How much did all this cost?"

Justus walked by her and hefted a bag. "I have an Aston Martin, a Mercedes, a Ferrari, and a collection of luxury watches, and you want to know how much a few plastic ornaments cost?"

She knelt down and picked up a sumo wrestler. "Maybe I'm just curious how much you thought this hideous thing was worth."

CHAPTER 5

Adam

ADAM MANEUVERED AROUND THE CORNER, the back tire of his motorcycle skidding over a patch of ice. The streets on this side of Cognito were recently sanded, but most areas were impassable. He needed to get to Silver's before dark, especially since his visor kept fogging up. He'd driven across a few snowy streets and had a few scary moments trying to stabilize the bike.

When he reached the flower shop, he pulled onto the sidewalk and parked beneath the awning. The best part about the city shutting down was the VIP parking. He tucked his black helmet under his arm and went inside, grateful when a rush of air warmed his face.

Man, going to the Christmas party was going to be awkward as hell. He'd almost declined the invitation since everyone there was either mated or related. Once again, he'd be sitting in a corner somewhere, watching.

The woman at the register gave him a rushed greeting. "I was just about to close up."

When he neared the counter and she noticed the scars on his face, her demeanor became guarded. Adam was used to it. A lot of humans associated scars with villains, and while Adam had done some bad shit in his life, he wasn't that guy anymore. He was just a Mage who earned an honest living as a Healer. He worked alongside Page, and their clients kept them busy, even though there were a few assholes who didn't think he could do a sufficient job because of his own injuries. Still, he wouldn't trade it for anything.

Adam put a friendly vibe in his voice and lowered his eyes so the older woman wouldn't hit a panic alarm. "I just came in to buy some flowers for a party. Do you think they'll fit in my backpack?" He turned a little to show her the long, empty backpack he was wearing.

She tilted her head to the side and steered her gaze toward the front window where his motorcycle was parked. "I can wrap them up in paper, but I can't guarantee they'll survive if you have a long way to go."

He scratched the side of his nose and looked around, overcome by the heavy floral perfume.

The woman appeared beside him and presented a pot of poinsettias. "This should do it. They're perfect for the occasion."

He cringed when he looked at the blood-red foliage. It was all wrong. "Mind if I just look around for a minute?"

Her gaze darted to the front window and then up at the clock on the wall. "They said a band of snow showers is moving in soon. I want to get home before dark."

"No worries, ma'am. I'll be quick."

Adam turned on his heel and studied the flowers inside the cooler, most of them roses. As he moved around the room, he approached a bouquet he couldn't take his eyes off of—one he knew would make an impression. "Do you think you can sell me these without all the purple flowers?"

She weaved around the tables and collected the vase of white daisies. "I can do that, but the price will be the same."

Adam didn't concern himself with bargains anymore. People had to eat and earn a living, so as long as he wasn't being swindled, he paid what was on the price tag.

After the lady plucked out the purple flowers and added a few more daisies to fill in the gaps, she emptied the water out of the vase and carefully wrapped the stems before rolling up all the flowers in cellophane. Adam didn't need the vase, and Silver had plenty lying around.

While the woman counted out his change, he took the flowers and carefully tucked them inside his pack.

"I had to cut the stems down a little so they'd fit," she said, handing him a few bills and small change. "I just don't know. Daisies can be so fussy. Good luck, and merry… happy holidays."

"Merry Christmas," he said, heading out the door.

The icy wind assailed him, and flecks of snow stuck to his neck. He slid on the warm helmet and cursed under his breath, wishing he'd worn something more waterproof than his brown leather jacket. Then again, he hadn't planned on taking this little detour.

Adam started the engine and eased onto the road. Snowflakes were sticking to his visor, and every so often he'd swipe his arm over it. He really needed to break down and buy a car, but man, nothing beat the freedom of a bike on the open road. Even out in crazy-ass weather like this.

When he finally reached Silver's building, he pressed his finger against the thumbprint scanner, and the underground garage door opened. Adam was on the approved list for garage access only; he didn't have permission to enter the building.

After parking his bike and setting the helmet on the back, he headed toward the doors and buzzed Lucian's apartment.

No one answered. Then he tried Levi.

"Come on. Someone answer," he grumbled.

When no one buzzed him in, he rang the intercom in the family room downstairs. While he waited, Adam kicked the sludge from his boots and dusted off his jacket. His jeans were saturated, and he wasn't sure if he could feel his legs anymore.

"Yes?" a bright voice answered.

"It's Adam," he said, uncertain to whom he was speaking. "I'm in the garage."

The door buzzed, and he went inside a stairwell that led up

to the ground floor. He reached a door and waited patiently. This one had a retinal scanner. *Justus and all his top-secret shit*, he thought to himself. It amused him—took him back to the days when he and his buddy Knox used to break through security systems like this.

When the door swung open, Adam was greeted by a fetching woman in cowboy boots and a knee-length blue dress with tiny white flowers. Sadie's blond hair was wavy and unkempt, and she had an untamed beauty about her that made him think of wild mustangs.

He leaned his arm against the doorjamb. "Life treating you well, Kitten?"

She smirked. "Come on in, Scratch. You're just in time for the ceremonial raising of the tree." Sadie spun on her heel and strutted away with a carefree swing in her step. "You should just see what—"

"Sadie?"

She quietly turned and centered her eyes on his. They were a milky green with flecks of orange, something Adam noticed every time he saw her. Sadie Cross was the baby of the family—born human and given up at birth to be raised outside their world. It was common practice among Chitahs, but fate had brought her back into their lives.

Maybe Adam had a little something to do with that.

Years ago, Adam had made a private agreement with Novis to offer her immortality as a Mage. He was certain her brothers wouldn't protest if it meant not having to watch her age and die, but they factored little in his decision. Adam had fallen in love with Sadie nearly the moment they met but kept it a secret. Novis agreed that after her thirtieth birthday, he would offer her immortality even though there was no guarantee she would accept. Adam's agreement with Novis had to remain secret or else Novis would rescind his offer. Novis felt it was important that Sadie not be influenced and that her decision was one of free will and not a condition of love.

So Adam backed off from pursuing her. He didn't want Novis to change his mind, thinking Adam was seducing her into their world. Despite how he felt about her, it was the right thing to do.

There was still a chance she might choose to remain human, and that possibility terrified Adam. Maybe unrequited love was the best way to protect his heart. Her friendship was enough, and besides, a gem like Sadie could never love a man like him anyhow.

Adam pulled off his backpack and unzipped it. "I got these. I don't know if they're still alive anymore, so you might want to put them in some water." He handed her the plastic-wrapped bouquet of daisies.

Sadie gathered them in her arms and drew in a deep breath.

A long stretch of silence passed between them, and he said so many things to her in his head.

Sadie swung her attention to Adam's old boots. "Where's your change of clothes? You're staying overnight, aren't you?"

He shrugged as they lingered in the hall. "Maybe."

She plucked a daisy out of the bouquet. "I'm keeping this one for myself, and Silver's going to love these. Daisies are a perfect idea for the table arrangement. Simple, classy… You're so thoughtful, Scratch. And you're totally staying overnight." She had a jaunty swing in her step as she strutted down the hall. "I'll tell Leo to lend you something to sleep in."

Adam snorted. "That's all right. I'll pass on wearing another man's pajamas."

She twirled the daisy between her fingers and gave him a coy smile. "Sleeping in the nude? That should be interesting if you're taking the futon downstairs."

Sadie moved briskly through the building, her wavy hair swinging back and forth and her boot heels clicking on the floor. Adam loved that woman and loved her hard. A beauty like her would never want a beast like him with all the scars on his face and body. Not that it mattered. He liked their relationship just as it was and didn't want to ruin it. Sometimes, when he wasn't working, he'd go to one of her shows and sit in the back to watch her play. Sadie had the voice of an angel and could stop a clock.

Just as she had his heart.

He didn't bother to tell her that he'd bought the flowers just for her; that remained his little secret. Sadie was a generous spirit and would have placed them on the dinner table anyhow to share them with everyone. That was just her nature.

Maybe next year.

CHAPTER 6

Silver and Finn

I WAS ABOUT TO COLLAPSE BENEATH a mountain of pies until Logan swooped in like the hero that he was and banished me from the kitchen. I took a short elevator ride downstairs to inspect the family room and see what needed to be done before it got too late.

The men had bought long tables and lined them up to the right of the door. Straight ahead, the leather couches were facing each other in front of the hearth. Usually the dark rug was in the center of the room, but someone had moved it closer to the fireplace, and the coffee table was parked in the corner by the door. The built-in bookshelves gave the room an inviting appeal, as did the fact that someone had moved all the lamps near the front by the game table, leaving the remainder of the room drenched in firelight.

I curled up on the sofa and draped a blanket over my legs. The log in the fireplace cracked like a whip as the fire gathered up momentum, radiating a heavenly warmth. Justus and

Simon had just assembled the plastic tree and were arguing about location.

"It's too close to the wall," Justus barked.

"Hurry up, Ghuardian. I'm dying to see what you've got in all those bags. You were a shopping machine today. The Shopinator."

He gave me a frosty glare with those blue eyes and then rubbed his bristly scalp. "The tree is crooked, Simon. Fix it."

"Who the bloody hell do I look like, Martha Stewart?" Simon appeared from behind the tree, a long green-and-red-striped elf hat on his head. "This thing is in four sodding pieces, and I'll be damned if I'm going to take it apart and reassemble it so it can meet your high standards. All you need to do is spin it around and no one will notice." He reached for the center pole and dragged it away from the wall.

The tree suddenly began to topple over, and Simon buckled beneath the weight of it.

Justus caught it, obscenities flying out of his mouth.

"Need some help over there?" Adam asked from across the room. There was nothing in his voice to indicate he was serious about helping so much as giving Justus a hard time. He was too busy playing backgammon with Sadie.

Justus dragged the tree a few feet forward and straightened it, but not before a branch thwacked him in the face. "Everything is under control."

I was facing the tree but couldn't see over the couch. "We

need to move the furniture," I pointed out. "You're not going to be able to see the kids opening their gifts."

Simon gave me a mirthless smile as he approached the sofa in front of me and shoved it around until it was facing the fireplace. "Problem solved. Anything else, love? Shall I repaint the walls or fetch your slippers?"

The door opened and Finn strode in, shaking snow off his hat. Lucian appeared behind him with an armload of boxes that he set down in the corner. Finn slung two plastic bags on the table and carried the rest to where I was sitting.

"Hey, sis." He collapsed next to me and reclined his head. He still smelled like snow, and I noticed a little sweat on his face.

I glanced at the trail of water he'd left behind on the floor. "Take your shoes off and warm your feet by the fire."

Without opening his eyes, he used his feet to kick off his shoes. "Never again."

"I feel you," Adam said from across the room. "It's a madhouse this time of year."

Finn sat forward and raised his voice. "A woman nearly called the police when the manager didn't have what she wanted in stock. Can't people just be grateful for what they have?"

I peered down at his bags. "It looks like you have a lot. Let me see the booty."

When Simon spun around and put his hands on his ass, I tossed a pillow at him.

Finn placed a sack in my lap. I reached inside and pulled out a long wall banner with snowflakes and cartoon characters. I refrained from smiling because Finn had never had a real childhood. He'd led a sheltered life, never exposed to the outside world. Even though the higher authority had employed him, he still dressed like a college kid and watched cartoons. Now that a few years had gone by and aged him, he looked more like a young man trying to hold on to his youth. We'd never pressured him to grow up and act his age. That would happen naturally in due time.

I mussed up his shaggy brown hair. "These are great. Did you remember to get napkins?"

"Yep. I also got pinecones that smell like cinnamon. Oh, and these red and green candles you can put on the table." Then he gave me a sheepish grin. "I know we don't have windows in here, but I bought these sticky things you can put on them shaped like snowmen and Christmas trees. I thought maybe the kids might have fun decorating the mirrors or walls later on." He raked his hair down to cover his ears, which stuck out.

"That's a great idea. I think you should show them how to do it. Maybe you should go upstairs and change out of those wet clothes. Your pants look like you waded through the Arctic Ocean."

He smirked. "I built a snowman out there for the kids to decorate later. I just hope Page has a leftover carrot."

I frowned. "Leftover from what?"

"Shit. Nothing." He shot to his feet and hustled out of the room.

I gaped at the tree. "What the hell is *that*?"

Simon poked an ornament, and I watched the giant plastic hamburger swing back and forth. "It's Christmas."

"That's not Christmas; that's lunch."

"Just wait until you see what else I've got in my little bag of tricks."

I stretched and got up, anxious to see what else they had bought. As long as there weren't panties and handcuffs, I was pretty okay with anything else.

When I peered into a bag, a laugh pealed out of me. "This is hilarious. Did you just grab random things off the shelf and run?"

"We handpicked everything," Justus said defensively.

Simon widened his stance and folded his arms. "I tried to get him to dress up as Santa, just to see what kind of chaos would ensue. I bet women would have knocked their children down to sit in his lap and pray they were on his naughty list."

Justus held out an ornament. "Do you want to do this instead?" he asked, trying to shirk his duties.

I shook my head. "I have complete faith in your abilities, but I'll be back to check on your progress."

"Don't wander far," Simon said in a singsong voice. "You'll miss the grand finale when we top the tree."

I patted Adam's shoulder as I headed out the door. When I reached the elevators, I found Finn sitting on the floor. I took a seat next to him and pulled up my knees. "What's wrong?"

His tone was sullen and quiet. "I can't explain."

"Is it the Shifter thing again?"

He didn't reply. Finn was an alpha wolf without a pack. He could pretend everyone in this house was a pack, but it wasn't the same as taking on a leadership role as a Packmaster. Not all alphas formed packs, but the instinct to lead was still there. Finn had greater aspirations to work in law. Even though the Cross brothers filled the void of what it must feel like to have packmates, we still weren't Shifters. Finn was alone, and I related to that feeling. No one understood my struggle with being a genetic experiment.

I rested my head on his shoulder. Finn didn't need to hear why he should be thankful or grateful. He already knew that. He just wanted someone to get what he was feeling and not place any judgment.

"It's not you," he finally said. "I don't want you to think it's you or Logan or anyone. It's me. I don't know. I can't explain it."

"Maybe if you found a nice Shifter girl, you'd have someone to talk to about it."

"I'm too busy to date."

Finn just wasn't emotionally ready. He'd been abused as a child and kept as a slave. The brand on his arm only served as a reminder that some people still saw him as nothing more than property. Finn was maturing before my eyes into a remarkable man, and as much as I teased him about dating, he needed more time. And Shifters had centuries of time.

"My wolf gets lonely," he admitted. "He paces and doesn't have brothers and sisters to howl with. It's not so much a pack he craves but companionship from another wolf. We've always been alone, but it just gets harder."

"It won't be forever," I said. "Someday things will change."

"You mean when I leave?"

I shrugged and sat up straight. "I don't know. We want you here, and this will always be your home, but it's also your life to live. You have to make choices for yourself. Logan says the fates brought us together for a reason. There's no telling what the future holds, but something will change. You'll see. Who knows, maybe you'll have a niece or nephew to take care of someday."

He draped his arms over his legs and smiled at me. "Any luck with that?"

"Not yet."

"If anyone deserves to be happy, it's you."

"I'm already happy."

Finn put his arm around me. "I know a few people. If you

two don't have any luck on the black market, I might be able to find someone who can help out."

"Thanks. Maybe we'll take you up on that someday. But for now, I think we need to hold off on the search. It's too painful, and I'm not sure if I can handle another disappointment."

"Sounds coolio. If it's meant to happen, it'll happen. If not, then screw it. Doesn't mean anything. You've still got Logan, me, and everyone else."

"Thanks, little bro. I think you're going to have to pull me up. My ass is glued to the floor, and my legs feel like cement."

He stood up and reached for my hands. "Why did you want to host this dinner all by yourself?"

I grabbed his hands and launched to my feet. "Because I want one Christmas where I feel like I had something to do with all the good memories. I don't want to just be the girl who brought the bag of chips or bowl of potato salad while Sunny or the Cross brothers served up a feast. It's my turn to show my stuff."

"If you need help, I won't tell anyone."

I pushed the button to my floor. "Bring the supply cart to my floor tomorrow morning. You can haul down the food and arrange it on the table. Just keep the foil on everything so it stays warm, and put the hot food on trivets."

"What the heck is a trivet?"

"You'll see. And don't forget to plug in the slow cookers."

"No problemo," he said, getting in the elevator. "Lucian's

volunteering his oven warmer if you want to shove anything in there."

"How about my head?"

CHAPTER 7

Silver and Logan

THAT NIGHT, I BEGAN PREPPING cold dishes like potato salad, Caesar salad, and deviled eggs. Max kept slinking around my legs in hopes that I'd drop something on the floor, so I locked him in the cat room to keep all his black hairs away from the food. Logan was still over at Leo's, gathering the desserts and taking them downstairs.

When a knock sounded at the door, I tossed the knife in the sink and wiped off my hands. My hair smelled like pie, my clothes had mayo stains, and my feet were killing me. When I opened the front door, my gaze drifted down to an adorable little blonde in a red-and-black dress.

"Rose, you're not supposed to be up here by yourself. Your daddy told you not to ride the elevators alone."

"It's okay. He gave me permission," she said. Rose had a better vocabulary than Sunny's twins, mostly because she was always trying to imitate the way her father spoke. "I have a present for you."

I noticed her hands were hiding something behind her back, and those big brown eyes were sparkling with anticipation. Rose handed me a thick piece of red construction paper folded in half. On the front, she'd colored a green Christmas tree and tried to draw a star at the top, which looked more like a nuclear explosion.

When I opened it up, the inside simply said: I LOVE YOU. The letters were distorted and extra big. Tears gathered in the corners of my eyes, and I bent down and gave her a big hug.

"This is so pretty, Rose. Thank you."

She kissed my cheek. "Thank you for all of Christmas. I can't wait for pie!"

I smiled and straightened her dress. "You look so pretty. I know Zoë and Knox are excited to come over in the morning and play with you. Aunt Sunny said they're going to sleep over tomorrow night. Doesn't that sound fun?"

She nodded excitedly.

Even though Knox was rambunctious and Zoë had a gregarious personality, Rose loved being around kids her age. They were as close as she could have to cousins or siblings, and since Rose was homeschooled, it was important for her to have that interaction with other kids. Otherwise she might end up becoming a little Justus, and I could only handle one of him.

I held up the card. "I'm going to put this in a very special place where everyone can see it. You better go back home before your daddy starts to worry."

"Bye, Aunt Silver!"

Her black shoes tapped on the floor as she ran back into the elevator. Hopefully she'd end up on the right floor. Rose knew her numbers, but sometimes she went to Uncle Levi's house to watch TV. Whenever she knocked on *our* door, Logan wound up escorting her home. Even though we lived in a secure building, he worried whenever he caught her alone. Justus and Page didn't have security locks to prevent her from leaving their apartment, and sometimes she snuck out.

I glanced out the windows into the darkness. Our view from the fifth floor was usually of twinkling lights in the distance, but the snow was so heavy that it was impossible to see across the street. I strode into our bedroom—just a large mattress on the floor in front of a window with a scenic view— and lay down on the bed. I held Rose's card close to my heart and wept against my pillow. Maybe it was the stress of the holidays, or maybe it was standing over a hot oven all day, but a flood of tears came, accompanied by a gripping pain in my chest, reminding me of how close we'd come to getting a child only to lose the opportunity.

How long would Logan be willing to endure this? I didn't even want to let myself hope anymore. Maybe he needed a child more than I did, and that thought hurt the most. We were kindred spirits, but what if that wasn't enough to keep us together? Despite every reassuring word he'd given me, I couldn't help but wonder if our love could weather this kind of storm.

It wasn't even a storm; it was more like a blizzard.

Little Rose standing at the door with that precious card reminded me of all the cards I'd never have on my own fridge. I'd never know what it was like to have a little one call for me in the middle of the night, to hear the sound of giggles while I sang, to give butterfly kisses and have tiny tears to wipe away. Being an aunt was a great experience, but it couldn't replace motherhood. A life without children flashed before my eyes and rocked me to the core.

The door flew open and hit the wall. A dark shadow entered the room and crawled across the bed, his warm body smothering my legs and a purr thrumming in his chest to console me.

I sniffed and peered down. "Levi, what are you doing here?"

He didn't speak.

That's how loyal the Cross brothers were. The scent of my devastation must have been potent.

I stroked my hand through his short hair and let him comfort me. Normally I wasn't the kind of girl who let a man drape himself over my legs, but I respected Chitahs, and this was a testament of how powerful our bond was as a family.

"Silver?" Logan entered the room and took in the scene. "Levi, leave us alone."

Levi quietly looked over his shoulder.

"Go, brother. I need to speak with my female."

Levi slowly rose and patted my foot before leaving the room, his eyes downcast.

When the door closed, Logan approached the right side of the bed and sat down beside me. He smoothed the tangled hair away from my face and held my gaze. "What troubles you?"

I handed him the card, and he opened it up.

After a thoughtful pause, Logan set the card on a short table by the bed. "I have failed you as a mate."

"What?"

He placed his hands on either side of me. "All these tears. I'm the reason. I should have stopped after the first time."

I cupped his strong face in my hands—a formidable face I had once feared long ago. Now all I saw when I looked at him was a devoted man who would move mountains for me. "I don't deserve you."

"No, you deserve better. I can't even find us a child. The world is filled with so many unwanted children, and I haven't been able to find a single one."

"Most of those unwanted children are humans. It's harder to adopt Breed children—you know that as well as I do. We both went into this knowing the risks." I stroked his chin with my thumbs, and Logan lowered his head to kiss them. "Finn says he might have connections. Maybe the black market isn't the way to go. It's wrong to bid for a child."

"It's a chance to save them from predators. I would rather

buy a child in peril than adopt one whose safety is certain." His voice fell to a whisper. "I would give all that I have to make you happy."

I sat up. "If you're doing this for me, stop."

He cocked his head to the side, his brows drawn together. "I'm doing this for us. Isn't this what you want?"

"Not if it means losing you. Maybe it's not in the fates for us to have children. I love you, but this could destroy us if we let it. I can imagine a life without children, but I can't imagine my life without you." My voice cracked.

Logan stretched out his long legs and pulled the covers over us. He surrounded me with his body and nuzzled against my neck. "I'll stop searching, and we'll go on as before. No more tears?"

I nodded against him. "No more tears."

His kisses against my neck grew insistent, and he slipped his hand down the back of my sweats. My lips parted, and I gasped when he rocked against me.

Logan released a throaty growl—one that told me he was going primal. Sometimes when we were intimate he'd flip his switch, losing all control to the Chitah instincts within him. He glanced up at me, his eyes as black as two ebony stones beneath moonlight. Logan was in there somewhere, sharing the experience with his inner animal. I kissed his mouth as my sweats and panties slid down.

"*Mine,*" he growled.

"Always," I whispered.

CHAPTER 8

Simon and Adam

"O I! WHERE'S SILVER?" SIMON SHOUTED. "Bloody hell, she's going to miss the unveiling." He could hardly endure the excitement any longer.

Adam set his beer on the fireplace mantel and held the stepladder for Simon. "Plug her in. We'll give Silver the full show tomorrow. I don't want to miss this."

Simon held a plug in one hand and the socket in the other. "Feast your eyes…"

As the power cords merged, the tree topper lit up and Sadie barked out a laugh from across the room.

A soft green glow illuminated the corner walls, and Adam stepped back to admire the sinister head of Mr. Grinch. A naughty smile curved up one side of the character's face, and a Santa hat covered his head.

"That's in Justus's honor," Simon announced, stepping

off the ladder, proud of his festive purchase. "I thought Silver would get a kick out of it. The resemblance is uncanny."

Adam patted him on the back. "She's gonna love it, but it might scare the hell out of the kids."

"Bollocks. He's smiling."

Adam chuckled. "That's the smile someone gives you before they cut your throat."

Simon strode toward the couch, murmuring, "You better be good for goodness' sake."

Simon took a seat and faced the fire, his arms draped across the back of the sofa, his leather pants creaking as he stretched his legs. There was a large box of sweets already opened, and the angel and devil on his shoulder were arguing on whether or not to leave it out for when the little ones arrived. The confectionaries were chocolate liqueur, and perhaps it would act as a narcotic and quiet them down. In his day, there was no such thing as a legal age for drinking. Simon didn't mind children so long as they belonged to someone else, but he did tire of hearing them prattle on about cartoon characters and pink unicorns.

Adam lifted his beer off the mantel and sat on the other couch to Simon's right. "You look like you're scheming. Where's Ella? I thought Silver invited everyone."

Simon pursed his lips and pretended he didn't care about Ella as much as he did. He had never announced their relationship since they were still figuring it out themselves, but everyone knew they were an item. He just wanted to take things slow since the poor girl had been through enough trauma, and entering a serious relationship with Simon Hunt was likely to scar her for life.

"She wants to be alone," he finally answered.

Adam arched his brow judgmentally. "Do you think that's a good idea on the holidays? Maybe you should send her a message and invite her yourself."

"She'd have to call a cab, and all that snow," he said, waving his hand. "No need to fuss. It's just a day like any other day."

The conversation died.

Ella found it difficult to be around families during the holidays since it only reminded her of her own loss. It seemed absurd to argue with that logic.

Still, it left him feeling sour about the whole affair. The shopping excursion with Justus had been a welcome distraction, but now that he was alone with his thoughts, he couldn't help but wonder if he should have just dragged her here by force.

An image flashed in his mind of her sitting alone by the window, a bowl of chicken soup in her hand and tears spilling down her cheeks while she watched the snow falling.

Bloody hell, he mused. *So* this *is what happens when you lose your testicles to Cupid.*

"Looks like it's you and me," Adam said. He raised his bottle in a toast. "Here's to the outsiders."

"I think we could change that with a little mistletoe."

Adam spit out his drink and wiped his chin.

Simon waggled his eyebrows and stood up. "Not me, you knobhead. *Her*," he said, jerking his thumb toward Sadie.

Adam turned as red as Santa's arse after sliding down a chimney. He shrugged it off as he always did and took another swig of beer. It hadn't escaped Simon's attention that Adam had an infatuation for Sadie. He was clever at hiding it, and no one else had seemed to pick up on it, but Simon began to wonder how much longer the charade could go on.

Since Chitahs could pick up emotional scents, Adam often distanced himself from her during social functions, especially when Levi was around.

"Should be an interesting dinner," Simon murmured as he sauntered off and took a seat across from Sadie. "How's it going, love?"

Sadie plucked another string on her guitar and adjusted the tuner. "It would be better if I had some new strings."

Simon hadn't bought gifts for anyone. His humor and good company were gifts enough. "How's the hippie lifestyle treating you?"

"You know, I'll be glad when I can get my own living space." She slid her pick between the strings on the bridge and leaned the guitar against the wall. "I'm more creative late at night, and I can't exactly practice whenever I want. It wakes Leo, and he's a guy who sticks to a schedule. At first we worked something out, but I feel like I'm suffocating my muse if I have set working hours. That's not how a creative mind works, and I really need to focus on new material. There's a band down in Tennessee who has an online album sold exclusively to Breed. I'd like to do something like that."

Simon heard Sadie's boot heels tapping against the floor. "Is the pay really worth it to keep singing in pubs? You've been wearing those same tattered boots for years."

"Hey, these are my lucky heels."

Simon snorted. "Planning on getting lucky tonight?"

A soft pink tinted her cheeks and she leaned back, giving him a smarmy grin. "You're not my type."

"I didn't mean me, and I think we both know what I'm talking about." Simon stood up and leaned toward her, smiling wolfishly. "Don't stay up too late waiting for Santa. He might not be the only bloke with a big package. See you on the morrow," he said with a wink.

CHAPTER 9

Justus and Page

AFTER ADORNING THE TREE WITH ornaments and shiny garland, Justus finally headed up to his house. No amount of calisthenics could have prepared him for holiday shopping and assembling a Christmas tree. Every time he closed his eyes, he saw twinkling lights and tacky sweaters.

Justus removed his shoes in the dark hallway, and his bare feet whispered against the kitchen floor as he strode into the living room and found Page asleep on the couch. He quietly approached, the streetlights reflecting off the snow and bathing the room in yellow light. Her favorite afghan was draped across her feet.

He loved it when her hair was messy and unkempt. She looked like a fairy who had wandered into his life and put a claim on his heart. One who blushed all over when he crooked his finger at her and whispered words of love in French. It was a language he didn't speak often, and he'd lost his heavy accent over the years. After Rose was born, he realized that teaching her French created a special bond between them and linked her to his past. He wanted to teach her everything.

Justus caressed Page's heart-shaped face and watched her long lashes flutter. She looked more beautiful now than when they'd first met, and not a day went by that he didn't thank the fates for bringing her into his life.

What had he done to deserve such a remarkable creature? She was not only the mother of his child but the keeper of his heart. An intellectual who worked tirelessly to counsel and heal people. She had postponed her appointments for two days in order to celebrate Christmas, and Adam had volunteered to leave in her stead if someone had a life-threatening emergency.

Justus took the reading glasses out of her hand and placed them on the table. A small book of sonnets was resting on the floor, the pages open. Justus cradled her in his arms and gently lifted her from the sofa.

As he moved down the hall, he peered into Rose's room and made sure she was asleep. She sometimes woke up in the middle of the night and would switch on a flashlight beneath the covers to look at her science books. She couldn't read anything that advanced, but she was an astute child and had recently asked Justus to teach her the alphabet and basic words.

She was so much like her mother.

He felt a pinch of nervousness again. Would she like his Christmas gift? Justus had taken great care to pick out something he thought would spark her imagination: a custom-made projector that displayed realistic moving images of stars, nebulas, solar systems, gasses—all of it. A friend of his designed gadgets for Breed that humans didn't have, and nothing he'd seen on the human market matched the realism of this light display.

Satisfied that Rose was asleep, he continued walking to his bedroom.

When he reached it, he nudged the door shut with the heel of his foot and walked forward. Without windows or a light, he counted the steps until he reached the bed against the left wall. Once there, he gently placed Page on the mattress and then strode to the dresser on the opposite wall to light a candle. The mellow light cast a spell in the room with its silent presence.

Justus liked the familiar, and when they'd moved into the new building, he'd wanted a simple room just as his others had been. Windows in the bedroom were intrusive and removed all privacy, not to mention security, so he'd taken it out. Page could have complained, but she understood his needs and didn't find it to be a huge sacrifice. They didn't quarrel over living space or material things; they compromised.

He carried the candle to the right side of the bed and set it on the table. Before getting in, he pulled down the covers to the foot of the bed and tucked her legs beneath them. A recent HALO case was on his mind, but he pushed the thought aside to lie next to his woman. No interruptions, no appointments, no talking about work.

He nestled on his right side, resting his hand on her stomach. He missed the feel and look of her swollen belly from when she had carried his child—how womanly she'd looked, how stunning. She'd glowed with a light that shone from within. The chain he'd kept which allowed him to be intimate with Page without his energy hurting her hadn't done anything in the way of bringing more children. Not that it mattered. Rose was enough.

"Can't sleep?" she murmured, eyes still closed.

"I'm displeased about the tree."

She smiled, tiny lines appearing at the corners of her mouth. "I'm sure it's beautiful, and I can't wait to see it."

"I'm not good at such things. There were too many choices. Simon became a distraction."

The sheets rustled when she turned on her side. "Did you take the presents down?"

"Yes."

"Just for Rose," she said firmly. "We promised not to get anything for each other. This is just for the kids."

He kissed the tip of her nose. "*Oui, mon ange.*"

"So… I'm thinking this is the year."

He raised his head and propped it in the palm of his hand. "For?"

"You know."

He knew, and his heart leapt at her revelation that she was ready to become a Mage. He would no longer have to worry about simple things like infections, disease, or even a slip on the ice taking the woman he loved. Novis had agreed to make her a Mage, but they hadn't ironed out the details. Normally Learners had to live with their Creators, who oversaw their training and education, but Justus had spent the past few years making sure that Page received the same kind of training and education he'd given Silver in hopes that it would sway Novis to relinquish his role and allow her to live independently.

"Can you speak to him?" she asked. "See if there's some kind of test I have to go through to meet his requirements. I don't want to live with Novis if that's the deal. I realize that's the Mage way, but this is my home, and I can't leave my family behind. Especially Rose. Every day watching her grow is precious to me."

"And you are certain you are ready? Is this what you want?"

He couldn't bear the thought of outliving the only woman he cherished, but ultimately the choice was hers.

"You are my forever home, Justus. Of course it's what I want. I just wasn't ready until… well, after the car accident. It reminded me how unpredictable life is. One minute you're here, and the next…"

He brushed a swath of her honey-brown hair away from her face and got lost in her dark eyes. They stood out, so wide and expressive. The same eyes he saw in their daughter. He was glad Rose had only inherited his blond hair. A little girl had no business resembling a brutish man like Justus.

"Plus I'm going into my thirties," she continued. "I'm getting older than you."

Justus smirked. He'd stopped aging at twenty-seven, but life was hard in those days, so he didn't look as youthful as most modern men. He liked what a few years had done to Page, adding some character lines here and there.

"I will speak with him," he finally said. "We'll work something out. I will not allow you to move in with him; that is not an acceptable compromise. Novis is a fair man; he will understand. You've also made progress with your education and training. The only thing that will change is learning how to use your gifts."

Page touched her finger to his lips. "I'm a good student, Mr. De Gradi. If I can endure five hours with you as my coach, I can do *anything*."

He pulled her close, kissing her soft lips, which tasted of sweet fruit. "Anything?"

Page coaxed Justus onto his back and straddled him, her delicate fingers splayed across his bare chest. "Let me show you just how firm these thighs are, *coach*."

CHAPTER 10
Simon and Ella

S IMON STRETCHED OUT ON THE leather sofa, the warm firelight cocooning his body. He stared vacantly at the colorfully wrapped presents beneath the tree. Simon had grown up in England in a century when poverty was rampant. As a boy, he'd visit upscale neighborhoods at Christmastime and listen to the sounds of merriment inside as families gathered to celebrate, sing carols, or play the piano. Then he would return to his own home to find his father passed out drunk. A stranger had once taken pity and given him a sixpence as a charitable gesture, but Simon hadn't used the money to buy himself candy or a good knife. He'd bought food.

When he grew older, he worked for aristocrats and experienced firsthand how the elite upper class celebrated their holidays. Yet the lavish production had never appealed to him. Even after becoming a Mage and earning a good living, he never saw the point. Christmas had turned into a marketing machine where children were spoiled with gifts and people stressed over the cost of things.

A decent bottle of wine and good company were all a man needed.

The tree had a modest number of gifts below it. A few small packages, something large tucked in the back, and a stocking for each child hung above the fireplace. Justus had dropped a few pieces of candy into them... along with an orange.

Adam was asleep on the sofa facing the fireplace, and every so often a snore settled in the back of his throat. It was after midnight, and Simon had been listening to him sawing logs for the past four hours.

He stretched his legs, relieved he was out of the leathers. Long johns, wine, and a toothbrush were the only things he'd brought over. He glanced down and admired his body, which measured a hair over six one. "Not bad, if I do say so myself," he murmured. While he kept his abs toned, Simon didn't bother bulking up his muscles as a means of intimidation. He liked the flexibility his physique gave him during knife fights. The ladies certainly liked what they saw. Although, since meeting Ella, he hadn't been intimate with anyone else.

She'd changed all that. Neither of them had made a formal declaration of monogamy, but Simon no longer desired other women. She fulfilled every need he had in a companion without it feeling all domestic and full of rules. They curled up together naked and actually talked.

Talked!

Simon was a sexual man, and yet no woman had ever wanted to stimulate his intellect as well as his cock. They played games, watched movies, and for the first time in his life, he felt a genuine connection to a woman on a level he hadn't thought possible. They'd hit the brakes on their relationship and just let whatever existed between them develop naturally. No expectations. No promises. They kissed, flirted, trained long hours together, laughed until their sides hurt, and…

Why the bloody hell had he left her alone on Christmas?

Because he was a sodding bastard, that's why. Deep down, Simon could never be the hero—the guy every woman fantasizes about settling down with as a permanent companion. Ella was young and would soon discover how many men would do anything to please a woman like her. Defects like deafness weren't an issue with everyone, and she had overcome many obstacles by learning how to read lips.

His phone vibrated. When he glanced at the screen, he typed out a reply to the message.

> Ella: I need your help.
> Simon: First you lift the lid, then you put the dirty clothes in.
> Ella: I'm trapped.
> Simon: What??
> Ella: My cab driver abandoned me. The snow is heavy, and I don't know where I am.
> Simon: What street?

Ella: Do you know where Tony's Pizza is? I'm across the street.
No one is open. I'm freezing. No heat.
Simon: I'm coming for you.

He leapt off the sofa and shucked out of his long johns. *Adam will get an eyeful if he wakes up,* Simon mused.

He yanked up his leathers, threw on his shirt, and searched the room for his socks and boots. The snow was probably piling up. The city trucks and plows didn't clear all the roads, and she'd never make it here without help from him. Ella had only visited Silver's house a few times, and this wasn't a side of town she was familiar with. Tony's Pizza was in the Breed district where a lot of juicers hung out.

That made him haul ass just a little bit faster as he put on his jacket and rushed out the door.

———————⁓~⟡~⟡⁓———————

When Simon turned right on Parker Lane, he discovered the streets were impassable. His car wasn't going to push through three feet of snow, so he pulled over and got out. Sleet pelted his cheeks as he turned around, the street visible due to the lights reflecting off the snow.

None of the roads that led to the pizza place were clear, so he had no choice but to walk. The snow was packed, so at least his feet didn't sink to the bottom in all places. He cursed under his breath as he trudged through the snow. Some spots weren't bad, while others had snowdrifts that piled on top of the cars. Simon was blessed to be tall enough that it only came up to his thighs, but his arse was still freezing.

After thirty minutes of marching through snow, his face was flushed, his legs sore, and his throat parched. Had there been a pub nearby, he might have broken the windows and sat down for a pint.

He neared an intersection and noticed a yellow cab on the left side of the road, facing the wrong way. The snow surrounding it had been stamped down, and the windows were fogged over. Simon rapped his knuckles on the glass.

Ella opened the door and gripped his hand. *Get in!* she said in thought through the connection they shared.

He scooted into the backseat and felt his body collapse with exhaustion. "It smells like old cheese in here. Why didn't you use your gift?"

This time Ella spoke aloud. "Where should I jump? On top of a building? A lot of good that does if I don't know where I'm going. Everything's closed, and all the streets look the same with the snow. I'm not even sure how to get back home."

She unzipped a small bag and pulled out a shirt. Instead of putting it on, she used it to dry his hair, soaking up the wetness on the ends as she scowled at him.

Her reproachful look amused him immensely. Even though they spent a lot of time together, she still lived in a separate apartment on the same floor, enjoying the freedom of her newfound independence. Everyone needed to experience that feeling. Before he'd left, Ella had remarked he wasn't dressed appropriately for the weather and he needed something warmer than leather pants. But Simon preferred making an impression. Real men didn't wear puffy jackets and earmuffs.

Ella reached down and unlaced his boots. Once she managed to get them off, she stripped away his wet socks and flung them against the back window. His feet were cadaverous in color, so he wiggled his toes to get some blood down there. She put a pair of her dry socks on him, which tested the tight fabric and stretched it to the point of no return.

He chuckled at the pink and black stripes. "I feel like Santa's elf. Wait till you see the hat I bought."

She glanced up at him at the tail end of his remark. "What?"

Sometimes he forgot she was deaf and couldn't tell when he was speaking to her or himself. Not everything said is meant to be heard.

After putting his boots back on, Simon pulled her close against him and touched her hand. "We need to leave before someone notices I left my keys in the ignition."

She looked down at her dress and black stockings. "I dressed up for a party, not walking in snow."

"You mean to say you didn't heed your own advice?" He bit his lip to conceal a smile and rummaged through her bag in search of clothes for layering. "What all do you have in here?"

Her eyes went wide in horror, and she tried to wrench it away.

Simon lifted a sexy red nightie and blinked in surprise.

She snatched it from him and stuffed it back in the bag.

Normally that's where he'd slip in a snarky comment, but Simon was gobsmacked. That wasn't the kind of outfit a woman wore when she had sleep on her mind. They'd never been sexually intimate. He and Ella were cut from the same cloth, and she needed time before she was ready for that kind of closeness. But they'd shared light, which connected them on a level that was safe and equally satisfying, if not more. Had Ella planned on consummating something between them tonight? If so, that was going to be an awkward scene with Adam three feet away.

Deciding this was no time for discussing lingerie and sexcapades, he handed her a pair of stockings and a red sweater. "Put all this on. And these slipper socks."

"I won't be able to get my feet in my shoes," she said, eyeing the thick material.

Simon lifted his hip and removed his dagger, slicing holes in the ends of the socks. "Wear them on your arms." Then he stared at her beautiful ginger hair, which was braided back. Her ears were bright red, so he removed his jacket and stripped off his T-shirt, handing it to her. "Tie this around your head."

She looked at him wide-eyed. "You'll freeze!"

Simon chuckled. "This is child's play compared to what I've seen, love. Do you have any bags in the trunk?"

She shook her head, so they exited the vehicle. Simon put his jacket back on and hooked the strap of her bag over his shoulder as he scanned the area to make sure they were alone. Before leaving, Simon memorized the cab driver's vehicle number and decided he'd pay him a visit later on to thank him for abandoning a young woman and leaving her to the elements. He held her against him as they retraced his steps back to the car. The walk was easier this time since he'd carved a path, but the air was so thin and frosty that it hurt to breathe.

It was an arduous walk, and Ella began to struggle as the snow deepened. She was seven inches shorter than him, but she never once complained or asked to stop and rest.

A flutter of dim energy touched his skin more than once. At first he blew it off, but the third time it happened, it was accompanied by a sound he couldn't discern. Simon gripped his dagger and whirled around with lightning speed, only to be confronted by... no one.

Except that in the distance, a shadow was fast approaching like ripples of water. Simon lowered his eyes and squinted.

A little brown-and-black scrapper of a dog was bounding through the snow. When he noticed Simon had turned to look at him, he stopped in his tracks. The puppy howled and then whimpered but kept his distance. It wasn't a wolf, so it couldn't have been a Shifter. Just some mutt.

Ella hadn't seen it. She was bent over, adjusting the stockings on her legs.

Every so often during their walk, Simon glanced over his shoulder and noticed the animal still following them. Barely. It struggled whenever it reached a deep wall of snow.

Tenacious little bugger.

Finally he spotted his GTO up ahead. There was a light dusting of snow on the roof, but nothing that would stall their drive home. When he looked back again, the puppy was nowhere to be seen.

Simon tapped Ella on the shoulder. "Warm up the engine."

She read his lips and then eagerly hopped in the car.

Simon stalked back the way they came, each step a regretful one.

"What the bloody hell is wrong with you? Since when did you grow a heart that bleeds for puppies? Next thing you know, you'll be helping old ladies across the street and donating to the Girl Scouts."

The least he could do was put the mutt in the backseat of someone's car or on a porch step away from the snowy street. It was likely to get squashed beneath a snowplow. Simon's boots noisily crunched on the snow, so he stopped for a moment when he thought he heard something.

A desperate whimper sounded from below. He squatted down and shoveled the snow aside with his hands, revealing a wet, shivering puppy curled up in a ball.

"Don't you belong to some chubby-cheeked little boy with a scooter?" He sighed, a cloudy breath thickening between them. "Well, don't just sit there freezing to death. Don't you have survival instincts?" He lifted the scrapper and held him against his chest. When Simon stood up, the little puppy licked his chin.

For pity's sake.

Simon unzipped his jacket and tucked the shivering puppy inside before zipping it back up again. "Now don't you go nibbling on my piercing. And try not to pee on me."

He headed toward the car and sat in the driver's seat. The heater generated more noise than warmth. Ella removed the T-shirt from her head and used it to soak up the water on her thick stockings.

Simon tapped her shoulder. "Brought you something."

Her eyes brightened when he unzipped his jacket and the puppy tumbled out.

"Oh my goodness!" She collected the wiggling furball, his tail wagging excitedly and his tongue cleaning her face. "Where did you find him?"

"A jolly fat man in a red suit."

CHAPTER 11

Silver

BEFORE DAWN, I DRAGGED MYSELF away from Logan's warm embrace and got ready. Since I had a busy day ahead of me, I ditched the fancy dress and put on a comfy pair of jeans and a red shirt.

Hours later, I'd found my groove. I had a turkey going in Levi's oven as well as ours, and I'd prepared everything for the cornbread dressing and side dishes. Homemade mashed potatoes seemed like too much work, so I decided to use the instant stuff in the box instead. A lot of things just required heating up, such as the peas, canned corn, and the rice I'd cooked the night before.

After buzzing Sunny and her kids into the building, Logan and I headed downstairs to greet them. Logan carried a bundle of small blankets in his arms in case the children were cold and wanted to snuggle up by the fire. Before my shower, I had snuck downstairs and put a few extra gifts under the tree and in the stockings, although by the look of things, Santa Justus had already paid a visit.

When I made it to the family room downstairs to greet Sunny, my eyes widened.

Levi and Lucian were setting breakfast on the table.

"You did all this?" I asked, ready to tackle them in a bear hug.

Lunch and dinner had been my sole purpose, so I'd failed to consider that our guests might be hungry at breakfast time.

Levi planted a big smooch on my cheek. "We've got your back. You do lunch and we'll take care of breakfast. I'm ready for this eat-a-thon."

Sunny, wearing a purple scarf and matching hat, followed Logan into the room. She gave me a tight hug. "Hey, sis."

"Merry Christmas, Sunshine."

She backed up a step and looked around. "Geez, it looks *amazing* in here. When did you have time to do this?"

"All credit goes to the boys," I said. "Rose should be down in a little bit."

"Hi, Aunt Silver!" Zoë said, peeking around her mother.

I crouched down and opened my arms. "Come give me a squeeze."

She giggled and wrapped her arms around my neck. Zoë was the spitting image of Sunny with her sparkling blue eyes and rosy cheeks. Both had blond hair, but Sunny's natural wave couldn't compete with Zoë's pretty curls.

And then there was Knox.

"Bang!" He fired his finger at me, and I collapsed on my back. Knox snickered and peered down at me. "You're silly."

I opened one eye. "Are you strong enough to help me up?"

His lips pressed tight, and with a look of determination, Knox grabbed my arm and pulled as hard as a three-year-old could. When I finally stood up, I bent down and kissed his forehead. As usual, his ears turned bright red, and he dashed across the room to check out the stockings at the fireplace.

"Greetings," Novis called from the doorway. He was dragging a red sack behind him that looked stuffed with presents. His black hair was more disheveled than usual, probably from carrying one of the kids and them messing it up.

Sunny wandered around the table and began filling a plate.

"That's quite a bounty," I remarked, greeting Novis with a smile. He wasn't a huggy-kissy kind of guy, and aside from that, he was my boss.

He bowed politely. "We also brought gifts for Rose. Nothing extravagant. I wouldn't want to offend Justus. Sunny wanted to leave some of the gifts behind and open them later so it wouldn't be so many, but I think she was just on the wrong bed when she woke up."

"I think you mean she woke up on the wrong side of the bed. Here, I'll put them under the tree. Make yourself a plate and sit down. There's a pot of coffee on the buffet table, and Levi brought down a microwave in case anyone wants cocoa."

I dragged the sack over to the tree and leaned it against the wall. No sense in pulling all the gifts out and torturing the kids since we weren't going to open them until later.

Knox squeezed the green stocking with his name on it.

I took his hand. "Honey, you're going to squish all your candy. Let's save the surprises for later."

He took off like an airplane toward the table. Zoë approached the tree and touched a shiny ornament shaped like a cheetah.

That was when my eyes dragged upward and I noticed the Grinch's sneering face on top. I erupted with laughter. Simon must have bought that as a joke, but I doubted Justus found any humor in it. We all loved Justus and knew he had a heart made from sugar cookies, but it just happened to be buried beneath more than two hundred pounds of grouch.

After my laughter died, I noticed Adam asleep on the sofa. His shirt was wrinkled, and one foot was on the floor.

I sat down beside him and patted his leg. "Wake up, Raze."

He peered at me with one eye. "Can't you see I'm sleeping, woman?"

"We took the TV out of here for a reason. You're just going to have to be social today."

I looked at his scars, which were more pronounced with all the shadows and dancing firelight. I was glad he'd stopped trying to grow a beard to cover them up. In the Breed world, some immortals viewed scars as a sign of weakness, but I saw them as a testament to Adam's bravery. Lives were saved because he'd ignored his own injuries in order to help others.

"You can go to Lucian's house and wash up. Breakfast is optional, but they made a casserole and a pot of coffee. And Adam? Thanks again for the flowers."

Adam sat up and stretched for a minute before he sleepily looked at me. "Merry Christmas, Silver."

We shared a look only old friends know about, the kind that makes you remember a different time when you were younger. Our lives had changed so dramatically since the night he rescued me. I thought about the man who'd looked after me like a protector even though we were strangers. Adam was a good-hearted man, and despite everything he'd been through between the accident and losing his best friend, he still remained a loyal, steadfast friend.

I gave him a hug and then pinched his chin. "You need a shave."

"So I hear. Where's your cat?"

"Max is banished from the party. I thought about bringing him down here, but he's liable to climb that tree and tear down the Grinch."

Adam chuckled and glanced over his shoulder as more people trickled into the room. After grabbing his backpack, he made a quick exit.

I scooted to the edge of the couch so Logan could sit to my right. The couches quickly filled, but Justus, Page, Sunny, and Novis all took the chairs by the tree, each with a plate of food in hand. Levi sat on the rug before me, one knee bent and a wide grin on his face while he watched the kids clapping their hands and squealing with anticipation. Uncle Levi was a favorite with the youngsters, and I had a feeling he might have hidden a few gifts of his own under the tree.

Leo strode in, the eldest of the Cross brothers. He bowed in greeting to all and sat on the far right sofa. "How is everyone this morning?"

"Wiped out," I said. "There's plenty of food coming, so don't fill up on breakfast."

He smiled with his eyes and stroked his reddish beard that looked more like an overgrown five-o'clock shadow. "You needn't worry about that. Not where the Cross brothers are concerned."

"Amen," Levi said. "My appetite runs twenty-four seven. Hey, Lo, you want a third helping?"

I glared at Logan. "*Third?*"

He looked at the empty plate on his lap. "Levi is mistaken."

"You're a terrible liar." I peered over the back of the couch and did a head count. "Where's Simon?"

Logan took out his phone and sent a quick text. "He says he went out for a stroll and he'll be back in a minute."

Sunny looked at her watch. "Should we wait?"

"Where are Kane and Caroline?" I asked. "Aren't they coming?"

Sunny wiped the corners of her mouth after biting into a biscuit. "They're snowbound. Lucky for us, Novis hired someone to plow a trail all the way here. I didn't realize how bad it was until I saw the news this morning. Kane doesn't want to risk it since they have so many overpasses on the way here. He tried to get the car out of the garage, but the city hasn't sent anyone out to their side of town, so it looks like a winter wonderland."

"We'll do an Internet chat later," I suggested. "Logan's laptop has a nice built-in video camera. It'll be like they're here."

"That would be great! I invited them over for New Year's, so they're going to stay with us for a few days."

"Ho, ho, ho," Simon boomed.

Everyone turned their heads. Simon strutted in, his leathers wet, his cheeks and hands bright red, his hair damp, and a pair of pink-and-black-striped socks on his feet. He tossed his boots aside and crossed the room to join us.

"What happened to you?" I asked.

Page shot out of her seat when she caught sight of Ella. "Are you all right?"

Ella's pale face was mottled with red marks on her cheeks, and her leggings looked wet. Tangled pieces of red hair hung askew, and her black eyeliner had smudged.

"Ella decided to join the party," Simon announced. "We ran into a little snag." When he squatted near Levi and unzipped his coat, something jumped out.

"A puppy!" the children squealed in unison. Three excited children crawled toward him, their giggles confusing the puppy, which began barking and turning in circles.

Simon rolled onto his back and collapsed, his arms and legs spread wide. "If anyone is in the spirit of giving, feel free to get naked and smother me with your body."

Levi chuckled and stood up. "I'll go make you two a cup of coffee with a little Irish cream."

Ella sat by the fire, her knees drawn up and arms wrapped around them.

Justus watched her shivering and shared a private look with Page, who nodded and stepped back. Justus then sat beside Ella and put his arm around her. She recoiled at first, warily looking up at Page.

But I knew better.

Justus wasn't hitting on Ella or giving her a friendly hug; he was turning on his internal thermostat and cranking it on high heat. Sitting near Justus was like snuggling up with a hot blanket that just came out of the dryer.

Ella leaned into him and withered like a flower in the hot sun.

"I'm next," Simon murmured.

"You can freeze," Justus retorted. "What were you thinking?"

Ella leaned away and looked up at Justus. She must have felt his chest vibrating and wanted to know what he was saying.

Simon rolled on his left side and propped himself up on his elbow. "Would you rather I left her to freeze in the back of a taxi cab?"

"Where was the driver?"

"He took off," Ella said, following their conversation. "He called someone and then told me he'd be back."

Justus clenched his jaw. "I bet that pathetic little worm lived nearby and went home. What was the cab number?"

"Justus," Page said, her tone a warning. "Let's open presents before we organize a manhunt."

CHAPTER 12

Justus

J USTUS HAD NEVER FELT SUCH contentment as he did seeing the children's faces light up while they opened presents. Ribbons and shiny paper were littered beneath the tree, and Knox was chasing the puppy around the room like it was his new favorite toy. Sadie strummed a soft melody on her guitar while everyone conversed and sipped hot coffee. Zoë had new barrettes in her hair, which she was showing off to everyone. Rose, not as hyperactive as the other two, was content to sit still and play with her toys.

Silver had excused herself to baste the turkeys and finish preparing lunch. Logan followed behind and stated as fact that he was helping her for the remainder of the day. Justus chuckled as she balked at Logan's offer and flashed out the door ahead of him.

Page leaned back in her chair by the hearth, encased in an enchanting aura of rich gold and shadows from the firelight.

Justus reached behind the tree and retrieved a box. "Rose, I have another gift."

She set down a doll and looked up with expectant eyes. After tearing away the red paper, she looked at the box. "What is it?"

He knelt down and rubbed the tattoo on his right arm. "It lights up on the ceiling. At night you can look at the stars."

Maybe the gift was too mature or too boyish for Rose. Sometimes he forgot that maybe little girls just wanted to play with dolls.

His heart sank when she pushed the box away and stood up. It shouldn't have mattered what a small child thought of his gift, but Justus was new to fatherhood.

But then Rose wrapped her arms around his neck and whispered, "I love you, Daddy."

"I love you too," he whispered back.

"Can I play with it now?"

Justus let go and pinched her cheek. "Let me set it up, and you're not to touch the machine or the cord." He opened the box, pulled out the projector, and searched for a socket on the nearby wall.

Page and Novis noisily cleared away the torn paper and ribbons, stuffing them into a large trash bag.

After tucking the cord beneath the rug so no one would trip over it, Justus set the projector on the floor and switched it on.

"Whoa!" Knox exclaimed from across the room. He ran over, his eyes looking up at the ceiling.

Sunny caught him just in time as he stumbled over the edge of the carpet. "Slow down, little man."

Justus tossed a few blankets and oversized pillows onto the floor. The children gathered around and passed out the stockings. They turned onto their backs with chocolates in their hands and dreams in their eyes as they watched a visual display of supernovas, colorful nebulas, and stars twinkling across the ceiling.

Novis sipped his merlot. "Mind if I ask where you bought that?"

Justus chuckled. "It was a custom job, but I'll give you his number."

"Very clever. A gift that makes them lie still."

Ella had fallen asleep on the couch, a blanket over her legs and her head resting in Simon's lap. She'd passed on breakfast, but not the glass of wine that Simon had offered to warm her up. It was good to see them together even though neither of them had made any public declaration about their relationship. Simon needed stability in his life, and a good woman has a way of making a man want to change for the better.

Lucian raised his arms and chanted a victory cry from the table where he was playing checkers with Finn. Sadie peered at them with mild interest while strumming a few chords on her guitar. It was the kind of melody that made a man want to sit with a glass of wine, close his eyes, and reflect on his life. Some of the tunes had been Christmas songs, but this was something he hadn't heard before.

"What are you doing?" Page asked when he reached behind the tree.

Justus pulled out a large, flat present and set it in front of her.

"What's this?" she whispered. "I thought we said no gifts?"

Justus didn't answer. He stepped around the children and sat on the sofa on the opposite side of the fireplace, watching anxiously. Instant regret settled in when she began tearing the paper at the top and then ripped it down the back. Maybe he should have given it to her upstairs.

Or not at all.

She had it facing the wrong way, and when she turned it around to remove the rest of the paper, her jaw slackened. "*Justus.*" Tears glittered in her eyes as she admired his gift.

Justus had spent months on the oil painting. He'd titled it *Mes Anges*. It was a portrait of a sleeping mother and child.

Page and Rose to be exact.

She covered her mouth.

"What is it?" Sunny asked. She walked over to take a look and then snapped her attention to Justus. "You painted this?"

He ran his hand over his bristly scalp and glanced up at the mirage of stars on the ceiling that held the kids spellbound.

Page tilted the frame for Sunny to grip and lurched to her

feet. His heart hammered against his chest as she closed the distance between them and sat on his lap.

She cupped his cheek in her hand. "My beautiful man." While her perfume was sweet, it wasn't nearly as sweet as the kiss she delivered.

An overwhelming sense of protectiveness flooded through him. A reminder that he'd die for this woman.

She traced her fingers over a pattern in his tribal tattoo that was hers—the one he'd woven in with the others. "It fills me with such joy to know you're painting again," she said softly. "You shouldn't hide that kind of talent. Maybe you think it belongs to the man you once were, but you're still that man. Just a little older. Maybe a little wiser."

He smirked. "Maybe?"

She curled up against him and chuckled softly. "A sumo tree ornament?"

"I'm glad the painting pleases you," he whispered.

Page stroked his jaw and kissed him on the mouth. "You please me."

Justus had learned over the years that Page couldn't be wooed with expensive things, unlike the women he'd previously been with. She preferred a book of poetry over a diamond necklace, or him cooking dinner over going to a gourmet restaurant. When she'd given him an art studio, his feelings about it were mixed. Painting reminded him of the man he once was before immortality and wars had changed him. Yet having his past collide with his future wasn't as catastrophic as he'd imagined it would be. It gave him quiet time to gather his thoughts and be present. Painting was once a respected profession, but now people thought such frivolities meant a man was too soft, and that's not the impression Justus wanted people to have of him.

"What are your thoughts on a nude portrait?" he asked.

Page snorted. "I'd love one of you. Maybe lying on a shag rug or—"

She giggled when he tickled her side.

"Simon!" Finn shouted. "I'm taking the dog for a walk. He left you a present by your shoes."

CHAPTER 13

Silver

J UST BEFORE NOON, EVERYONE WAS ready to eat. Logan set up a virtual chat with Kane and Caroline, and Sunny gave them a tour around the room before we set the laptop on a table and chatted with them for a while.

When I went upstairs to heat up a few remaining side dishes, Logan followed behind to load up the cart Finn had brought up. He had to make several trips to get it all down, and Levi helped carry the rest of it from his kitchen, including a small ham, which he was happily in charge of slicing.

Candles and hurricane lamps on the table and buffet table flickered, casting a magical spell on the room. The light sparkled off the crystal glasses and fine china, and silverware was placed on the folded napkins, ready to slice into the bounty of food that awaited us. The ham glistened, and the delectable smells from turkey, dressing, and pies wafted through the room. Everyone gathered at the table except for Knox, who was fast asleep by the fire. I had a clear view of him from my seat near the left end of the table.

Logan stood up and raised his glass. "To Silver… for making this occasion one that will live in our memories forever. To my family, which I consider each person sitting at this table to be, may you have a prosperous year ahead. May you all be blessed by the fates, and may we have enough wisdom to see the joy in our lives no matter what destiny we're given."

"Cheers," everyone said, their glasses clinking together.

Logan's speech inspired Leo to say something, and the next thing we knew, everyone was making a toast. Even Rose, who said, "I like everybody here, and I want pie for dessert."

An hour later, we had gone from serious conversation to laughter as we recounted funny stories, including the time a bunch of baby ducks followed Levi home, thinking he was their mother.

"Mmm, this is so good," Page said, working on her second helping. "I'm going to need a long nap after all this."

I laughed. "We haven't even touched dessert. I thought maybe after everyone's done eating we could clear the table and play games. Does anyone want me to put some coffee on?"

Lucian set down his glass. "I'll take care of it when I clear my plate. I've also got some imported beer if anyone's interested."

"Interested," Adam said, raising two fingers.

"Same," Levi said, also raising his hand. "No offense,

Simon, but wine knocks me out. I like to be lucid when I'm eating."

I raised my glass. "Not me. Pour me another."

"Give her the whole bottle," Simon said around a mouthful of dressing. "She deserves to spend the next three days unconscious. Bravo, love. You pulled it off splendidly."

Justus sat to my left at the head of the table and Logan to my right. Page glanced over her shoulder at the puppy, which was sleeping in a box Finn had made for him. All we could see poking out of the plaid blanket was his tail. It made me wonder if a pet might curb some of Finn's loneliness. Would a dog be the same as a packmate? Maybe it wouldn't be appropriate. Some Shifters had negative views about owning pets. Something to discuss with Logan later.

When I tried to shove another cooked carrot into my mouth and my stomach gurgled in protest, I put my fork down. "I think I'm officially done."

Logan swept my hair back and planted his warm lips on my neck, sending tingles down my body to all the right places.

Sadie rose from her chair. "Hey, you two. I have a surprise. Don't be mad."

I frowned. "Why would I be mad?"

She reached into a sack near the door and pulled out a tin. "I know you made desserts, but I figured I'd make a pecan pie. If nobody eats it, then I'll just send everyone home with a slice. No biggie."

Adam cleared his throat. "Slide that over by me and I'll guard it for a little while."

"Guard it with your mouth," Simon added.

Sadie walked to the far end of the table and set the pie in front of Adam. He smiled up at her and winked before grabbing a small plate.

Meanwhile, Justus was too busy eating a turkey leg with his hands to concern himself over pie. Page normally admonished him for bad table manners, but she sat across from me, her eyes glazed over as she stretched out a yawn.

Logan's phone suddenly rang.

I glanced down. "Who is that?"

"Be right back." He stepped away from the table and strolled toward the fireplace, his voice low.

"Can I play with my toys?" Rose asked politely.

"Go on," Justus said, watching her scamper across the room.

Finn reached over and pinched my arm. "Thanks for making those rolls. They were the bomb. We should do this every month."

I laughed. "Only if *you* do all the cooking. It *was* pretty great though, wasn't it?"

Levi handed his plate to Adam. "Give me a slice of that pecan. And don't be stingy—I want a big slice."

It warmed my heart that everyone had helped out in their own way, even though I had specifically told them not to. We had plenty of chips, dip, sodas, veggie trays, and fruit to feed us for days.

I rested my chin against my fist and looked into the dark room lit only by firelight and a one-of-a-kind Christmas tree. Justus had turned off the projector before dinner so it wouldn't overheat. When my gaze drifted toward Logan, I noticed him staring at the fire with his phone in one hand.

Levi drew in a deep breath and turned around. "Brother, what's wrong?"

When Logan stalked toward the table, I noticed the black rim around his eyes was wider than usual, swallowing up the gold. He stopped at Rose's empty chair and locked eyes with me.

I got butterflies.

When he spoke, his voice was low and serious. "I have to go."

"Go where? You promised not to take any jobs this week."

Levi and Leo simultaneously rose from their seats, their nostrils flaring. They were picking up a strong emotion, but I didn't need to be a Chitah to see that something was wrong.

"Logan?" I said, my heart thumping. "Go where?"

He bit his lower lip and averted his eyes. "I know we discussed this last night, but I still had an open bid. The auction closed."

I stood up. "What does that mean?"

"It means… there's a child waiting for us."

Chills swept across my arms. "Are you sure? Maybe it's a scam. Maybe they—"

"It's a live transaction. I have to make the exchange today or she'll withdraw the offer."

"It could be dangerous," Leo warned. "They might be luring you for money and using a woman to gain your trust."

Levi pressed his fingertips against the table. "Leo's right. You need to arm yourself."

I stepped back and pushed in my chair. "I'm going."

Several voices rose up in argumentative chatter, some mentioning the dangers of the snow while others were concerned about who we were dealing with.

When Justus seized my arm, I searched his eyes for some sense of understanding. "I have to go. You know I can take care of myself. I'm not letting Logan do this alone. I know it's dangerous, but this could also be our only chance."

Justus loosened his grip without a word. Only a father could understand how important this was to us.

Unlike some of the men in the room, Logan didn't argue for me to stay. We'd always done everything together, including fighting battles. If this was a setup to ambush him for money and take his head, I wasn't going to let that happen. But if this was a legitimate offer, I had to be all in, despite what we'd agreed upon the night before.

Simon polished off his wine. "You need backup."

"We can't risk it," Logan said. "My contact is already

jittery about the situation. I don't think she's done this before, and I'm afraid she'll back out. We can't come across as people with malicious intentions to steal the child without paying. I had to extend my trust in exchange for hers. No backup. No weapons."

I flashed upstairs as fast as I could, my heart racing inside my chest. Was this really happening? Or were my hopes going to be dashed once again?

I stuffed clothes into a bag for each of us. Toothpaste, toothbrushes, underwear…

"What else? What else?" I whispered, looking around the room.

Logan came into the bedroom. "We go now. There's a cabin upstate she reserved for us, and we'll meet her there. It's secluded, and I don't know how long it will take to get there with the weather. We might have to walk some of the way."

I snapped my fingers. "Boots."

Logan and I had quality winter gear, so I slipped on thermal pants beneath my jeans before grabbing my waterproof boots. Logan put on his black down coat with the fur-lined hood. I had a matching one except that it reached my knees. My mind wouldn't think straight, so I didn't bother packing anything else.

As I lifted our bags, Logan took me by the arms and kissed me hard. "It's happening, Little Raven."

"What?"

"Our destiny."

CHAPTER 14

Levi

L EVI GLANCED AT THE CLOCK again. It had been two hours since Silver and Logan left, and his nerves were a mess. He could barely enjoy his fourth helping of apple pie à la mode.

Sunny and Novis had talked about canceling their plans to stay the night until Justus convinced them the roads weren't safe enough to drive. The city trucks would be out the following morning, so there was no sense in putting the kids in unnecessary danger. There was plenty of room, and Page offered to lend them something to wear if they had to stay a little longer. After all, Sunny and the children were mortal, and that made them fragile. Had they insisted on leaving, Levi was pretty sure that he and Lucian would have removed the tires from Novis's car.

Levi folded his arms while listening to Sadie's sweet voice singing the children to sleep. They were snuggled up on the sofas with their blankets and stuffed animals, and their eyes were transfixed on the light display above. They could be a handful, and while some of the adults needed an occasional break from all the noise and excitement, Levi didn't mind. He liked the sound of children and the energy they brought into a house. It was a sound absent from his own home.

Leo was their only real hope for expanding the Cross family, and like most Chitahs, he was probably waiting around to meet his kindred spirit. If that didn't happen, he'd just have to settle with someone who could make his heart go pitter-pat. Logan and Silver obviously couldn't have children together, and Lucian was too damn introverted to become a family man.

Levi sighed and leaned back in his chair. It wasn't in the cards for him to have kids. He had a hard enough time finding men who were out with their sexuality, let alone a good match. The men he dated were outside his Breed. What was the point of dating another Chitah? Because of the social pressure to have kids, most of them didn't come out. They were treated as traitors who didn't care about their race surviving. Statistically there were more male Chitahs than females, and most waited as long as it took to find their kindred spirit—sometimes centuries, which was why there weren't as many as one might think.

He rubbed his face. Now Logan and Silver were in a dangerous predicament. Some of the criminals who worked the black market were honest, but Levi patrolled the streets and had once worked in a Breed jail. He knew all about that dark underworld. Children were rarely given up for adoption, and those who wound up in orphanages or on the black market came from tragic circumstances. Unless they were stolen. There were plenty of sickos who wanted children for sadistic reasons. Some used them as personal servants, and others selected kids of a certain Breed to do their dirty work. They raised Shifters and Chitahs to become killers who did their bidding. It was the ultimate form of brainwashing.

Fake auctions were often created to swindle the highest bidder. They would lure the buyer to an isolated area, take their money, and then murder them.

People disappeared all the time.

Lucian took a seat in front of him with a plate of vegetables and dip.

Levi glared. "How can you eat at a time like this?"

After crunching on a carrot, Lucian replied, "You seem to be suffering from pie amnesia."

Lucian was short for a Chitah, standing at five ten, and he was built more like Logan with his sinewy muscles and strong bone structure. His onyx hair was a little wild, but he had the same bright golden eyes as the rest of his brothers. Despite his shortcomings, he was definitely a Cross with his good looks.

He was also a smartass.

Lucian rolled a radish between two fingers. "They should have packed weapons," he said quietly. "Agreement or not, they could have hidden them in the car. He doesn't have a clue who he's meeting."

Levi shook his head. "He can't go in packing. If the woman's a Chitah, she'll scent he's lying. You know our word is our bond; Logan made a promise, and he can't back out of that."

"It could cost him his life."

"Lo can take care of himself. Silver's a pretty badass Mage. You've seen what she can do with lightning."

Lucian popped the radish into his mouth. "What if they're ambushed on the drive?"

"Are you trying to provoke me?" Levi growled. He stuck his finger into Lucian's onion dip and swirled it around.

"That doesn't bother me," Lucian retorted.

"You don't know where my finger's been."

"That's not the finger you pick your nose with."

Levi smiled. "You're right."

Lucian shoved the plate away. "Dammit. I'm just trying to work out the scenarios. This is our brother we're talking about."

Levi wiped his finger on a napkin. "Think I don't know that?"

"What are you two scheming?" Leo took a seat next to Levi. "I don't like the scent I picked up from across the room."

Levi ran his finger over the dimple on his chin. "I don't think we should have let them go alone. I know that's part of the deal, but—"

"It could also jeopardize their arrangement," Leo reminded them. He set his elbows on the table and rubbed his temples. Everyone looked to Leo for guidance. He was the eldest.

"Which outcome are you willing to live with, Leo? Preventing them from having a child or their blood on your hands? Maybe it's legit, but are you willing to take that chance?"

Leo shook his head. "I honestly don't know which would be a worse fate. You know children are impossible for them, and the orphanages have turned them away because they're an interracial couple. They think a Chitah and a Mage aren't fit to raise a child. The black market was their last resort."

Levi thought about walking in on Silver the night before and the absolute devastation he'd scented in the air. He knew it had something to do with the absence of a child, and while it had always been present during holidays and birthdays, this time was different. It was the first time he'd realized just how traumatized they'd become from all the lost chances.

He cursed himself for having told them to keep trying. Maybe he was partly to blame for constantly reassuring them that a child would come along eventually. That was wishful thinking. In the real world, things didn't always work out. Wishes didn't always come true. He knew that more than anyone.

Lucian tilted his watch. "It'll be dark soon. If we leave now, we can catch up."

Leo's eyebrows drew together. "Leave?"

Levi nodded. "Yeah. Leave. I bet Logan let the juice die on his cell phone. He can't even call for help."

"I looked up the location of the cabin on satellite," Lucian said. "A phone wouldn't make a difference. It's out of range."

"I can't just sit here," Levi complained. "My truck has a full tank of gas and brand-new snow tires."

Justus appeared at the table and sat next to Lucian. "I have de-icer, tire chains, winter gear, and a plow attachment if there's room in the back of your truck. Whatever you need I can provide. I'm with you. The longer I sit here and think about it, the more uneasy I am about the whole situation. There is nothing we can do to stop them, but there *is* something we can do to help."

Leo eased back in his chair, lines deepening in his forehead as he stared at Lucian's dip.

Levi leaned forward, his voice steady. "Come with us, Leo. Finn and Lucian can squeeze in the back."

"Finn may not want to go," Leo suggested.

"Go where?" Finn rounded the table and sat down.

Levi looked over his shoulder at him. "We're going after Logan and Silver."

"I'm in."

Leo locked eyes with Justus. "Will it ruin the celebration if we leave?"

Justus laughed. "Between the children and Simon, our

hands are full. Nothing is ruined. We'll still be here when you get back."

Levi stood up. "Then it's settled. We go."

Justus rose to his feet and clapped his hand on Lucian's shoulder. "I would accompany you, but—"

"No need," Leo said, picking up the same scent they all did: guilt. "You have a family to protect. We'll give you access to Lucian's control room. Someone will need to periodically check security cameras and make sure all the alarms are operational."

Justus inclined his head. "I only ask one favor: see that my Learner returns home safely."

CHAPTER 15

Silver and Logan

W E HEADED NORTH, BUT THE drive took much longer than it normally would have. Parts of the highway were treacherous where precipitation on the overpasses had turned into ice, and with the snow covering the streets, it became impossible to see the ice patches let alone the road. If it hadn't been for the mile markers and guardrails, we would have driven into a ditch. The city highways had been sanded, but the farther we drove into the country, the worse the roads became.

Between Logan and myself, we owned three vehicles. One was his old silver car, and that wasn't suitable for navigating wintry roads. Nor was mine. So we took the Chevy Tahoe, a joint purchase we'd made when we first moved into the building and realized family outings with the Cross brothers weren't possible in a sedan. Sometimes we'd load our camping gear into the back and head over to Logan's cave... for old times' sake.

As we drove to our destination, we worked as a team to navigate. Logan slowed the vehicle down whenever we neared a sign to make sure we hadn't passed our exit. There were a few abandoned cars on the side of the road, and each time we passed one, I looked closely to make sure no one was inside.

In the mad rush to leave, we hadn't thought to bring water. There were no businesses out in this neck of the woods, and the few we passed were closed. So at one point, Logan stopped the car and filled a thermos with snow. We melted it down, added more, and shared the cup. It wasn't the most ideal situation, but we had no alternative. While we weren't exactly going to die from thirst, the last thing we wanted at a time like this was to become dehydrated and weak, especially if we might end up walking.

I gripped the armrest when the truck went into a slide. Logan coolly controlled the vehicle, never once flinching or showing signs of panic.

"This is it," he announced, turning off the two-lane expressway and onto a rural road.

The sun must have gone down because the sky was growing dimmer by the minute. Logan flipped on the headlights.

"Looks like some of it's freezing," he said, pointing at the wipers.

The windshield was becoming a blurry mess, making it difficult to see. He switched on the defroster and leaned forward to concentrate. We didn't have tracks left behind by truckers to follow anymore, and if we slid off the road, we risked not reaching the cabin in time.

"What are you looking for?" he asked, noticing I was looking in the back.

"Do you think it's safe to carry all that money in a bag?"

He threaded his long hair away from his face. "She's not going to take a check."

We'd been putting aside our money in case we'd have to make a cash exchange, but we were still short and had to borrow some from Justus, even though Logan earned decent money as a tracker, and I wasn't doing too shabby as an apprentice.

"Are you cold?" He adjusted the heater before I could answer.

I wrung my hands. "No. How much farther?"

"According to the map, another two miles."

"Do you think she'll be there waiting?"

He shook his head. "I don't know. She said the cabin is ours for one night only, but it's under a false name. She doesn't want any connection with us."

"Who is she?"

"I don't know."

A deer emerged from the woods and stared at us wide-eyed as we passed by him and made a left. The tires struggled against the deep snow, and the trees grew taller and denser. There weren't any tracks ahead, so maybe that was a good sign that we weren't late. I was afraid if she got there first, she might grow impatient and leave.

"One more turn," he said, veering left.

We hit a bump, and the front end angled down. Logan suddenly threw the transmission into reverse and backed up a few feet. Once stabilized, he put the car in park and shut off the engine.

"I can see the cabin up ahead. I don't want to risk getting stuck since we can't stay for more than a night. This road is probably unpaved, so we don't have any traction." He put on a pair of black gloves. "We'll walk the rest of the way. Why don't you run ahead of me and get a fire going?"

"Alone?"

He zipped up his coat. "I have a snow shovel in the back. I should clear the road for her so she doesn't have any trouble getting in. I don't want the child to be frightened or get injured in a car accident we could have prevented."

I put on my down coat and got out. The wind was uncompromising, so I drew the hood over my head and marched toward the cabin. Logan left the headlights on to brighten the way since I wasn't born with night vision.

The snow at one point reached my waist, and I had to use my hands as a shovel and trudge through it. The closer I got to the cabin, the more the snow thinned out. The tree limbs were weighted down, and when I reached the porch, I stomped my feet to get the snow off my boots and jeans. My muscles ached, and despite the cold, I was sweating from the exhausting hike.

Talk about rustic, I thought to myself, getting a good look at the cabin. It might have shocked me that it was a rental had it not been for the fact that there were hunting enthusiasts who didn't care about amenities. It made it easy for owners who didn't want to be bothered with things like upkeep and maintenance costs.

Just as the woman promised, the key was hidden beneath the doormat.

When I walked inside, I searched in vain for a light switch. Unable to see very well, I shuffled to the fireplace on the left and searched until I found a box of matches. The first one snapped in half, and when I struck the second one, the tiny flame provided enough light for me to see a candle on the hearth.

I stood up, candle in hand, and surveyed my surroundings.

There were logs stacked against the wall by the fireplace, an area rug covered in dirt, and a plaid sofa facing the front door. On the right side of the cabin was what looked like a kitchenette, except the only thing in there aside from the counter was a woodstove and a sink that probably didn't work. I glanced up a ladder to the right of the sofa and guessed the loft was above the kitchen.

Talk about quaint.

Checking out the sleeping arrangements wasn't high on the

priority list, so I put a log on the grate and reached up to open the flue. To get the fire going, I wadded up some newspapers that were stacked in the corner and stuffed them beneath the log. At least the wood was dry.

Once the log was lit, I took off my coat and began the impossible task of pulling a Mary Poppins and making this cabin spotless. First I wiped down the floors and table with a rag I'd found beneath the sink. Since the plumbing wasn't working, I used the water that I'd tracked in. With a child coming, I wanted to get the place as sterile as possible. Most Breeds didn't catch human viruses, but Relics did. Who knew what all was on the floor or the last time someone had bled on it.

The fire crackled, and the wood floor and walls were suffused with deep amber from the firelight. As I polished the window, my heart leapt. I couldn't believe this was happening—that I was actually going to be a mom. A torrent of fears flooded my mind, like what if the child was afraid of us? Seeing a Mage and Chitah together wasn't common; we were natural enemies. If he or she was a Chitah, I might end up being their worst nightmare.

"Get it together," I muttered, realizing I could end up making the situation a lot worse just by fretting over every worst-case scenario. If the child was a Sensor, then we needed to keep our emotions in check so we wouldn't convey the wrong message.

The door opened.

"Wipe off your boots!" I shouted. "I just cleaned the floor."

Logan filled the doorway, his breath heavy as he scraped his boots across the doormat. "This is not what I expected."

I planted my fists on my hips. "You should have seen this hellhole an hour ago. Can you shake out the rug? It's full of dust."

Logan dragged the rug outside and knocked off as much dust as he could. He threw it over the railing and hiked into the woods before returning with a large branch he used to pound it out.

When my rag had turned muddy brown, I inspected the room.

Not bad. At least there weren't curtains to clean or other furniture to dust off. Even the musty odor was now replaced with the inviting smell of burning wood.

Logan returned and draped the rug in front of the hearth before he collapsed onto the sofa, a cloud of dust billowing around him. "The road's clear."

"And your face is red." I unzipped his coat and pulled it off. "There were two glasses in the sink. I melted some snow to clean them off and then filled them up if you're thirsty."

"What's wrong with the sink?"

I handed him the water and he gulped it all down. "Do I look like a plumber? The only other appliance is a woodstove, but we didn't bring any food with us, so it doesn't matter. What were we thinking?" I took the empty glass and set it on an end table. "What if they're hungry and she wants to stay a few hours? We might have to sleep here for another night because of the weather; it's not safe to drive in the dark. Especially with a child, and we didn't even think to bring a car seat!"

"Easy, Little Raven. Chinese food isn't the only thing I know how to hunt. We won't be going hungry."

When he dazzled me with his smile, I sat down and curled against him. No matter the situation, he always made me feel protected. I pinched the stretchy material of his long sleeve. The blue-grey color was one I loved seeing him in. Logan was deliciously warm from all the snow shoveling, and I rested my cheek over his heart.

He kissed the top of my head, his voice a soft caress. "Do you want to lie down?"

"I'm petrified to see the sleeping situation upstairs. There might be a critter living inside the bedcovers. Anyhow, I don't think I could sleep if I were given a tranquilizer."

"I could rub your feet."

I smiled against his chest. "You know me too well, Mr. Cross."

When my mind started racing with anxiety, Logan began purring. He didn't say anything, but I knew he was feeling the same way. Uncertain, excited, afraid, and hopeful. I wasn't sure how to comfort him in return, so I wrapped my arm around him and held him close.

We waited for what seemed like centuries.

We waited to meet our destiny and face it together.

And then a motor sounded in the distance.

CHAPTER 16

Sadie and Adam

BEFORE HER BROTHERS LEFT TO go after Logan and Silver, Sadie had made sure to pack them plenty of food and water in several coolers. Between the extreme weather and potentially dangerous situation with the black market negotiation, she wasn't able to relax for the rest of the evening.

"You're pretty quiet over here, Kitten."

She looked up at Adam, who joined her at the empty table. Page and Justus had carried the leftovers to Lucian's kitchen, except for a few desserts.

Sadie pinched the foil around a pie plate. "My whole family is out there, Adam. The only real family I've ever known. I should have gone."

"There wasn't enough room in the truck."

"Look at me, Scratch. I weigh a buck and a quarter. You could fit me in a glove box."

He smiled handsomely and dragged a small plate of carrot sticks in front of her. "You should eat something."

Sadie sat back. "Nah. It'll be time for dinner soon anyhow. Since Page and Justus did all the work taking it into the kitchen, I'm going to heat everything up and set it out. Parents should enjoy their time with the kids," she said, pointing at the group in the living room. Knox was playing with a toy truck, and the girls were coloring.

Sadie had a feeling Ella would help her with dinner. Ella meshed really well with their crazy makeshift family even though she was on the quiet side. She could speak, but she spent so much time following the conversations and lip-reading that she did better with one-on-one chats. Simon wasn't going to help, especially after polishing off a box of those little chocolate candies filled with alcohol. He was barely awake, one leg slung off the couch and a pillow over his face.

Adam munched on a carrot. "I'll help."

And that's just the way Adam was.

Sadie had liked him from the start, despite his gruff demeanor. Adam had endured a tragic past—one that changed his life. Not just because of the scars on his face and body, but the ones on his heart. Silver had mentioned that Adam was once a different man before the attack—less guarded and more social. Sadie had never known the old Adam, so she could only judge the man she knew now. The Healer who dedicated his life to helping others. The man who, despite his rugged appearance, knew how to waltz. A friend who always had your back and knew how to make a girl smile. Luscious brown hair, dark eyes, tall, a square jaw, classically handsome, mysterious, charismatic, and oddly single.

She furrowed her brow. "Why don't you ever date anyone?"

"Why don't you?" Adam crunched on another carrot, unfazed by her candor.

"Maybe I do."

"That's not what I heard."

Was that jealousy in his voice?

Sadie just smiled at him. Truth be told, she hadn't dated a man in years. Plenty of jokers had asked her out—it could hardly be helped in her profession. Guys saw her on the stage and created an image of who she was, and seldom did that idea ever match up with the truth. Nobody wanted to know the real Sadie, but none of that mattered. She had a good thing going with her music and didn't need a broken heart for songwriting inspiration.

Adam's gaze lingered a little too long on her hands, so she pulled them onto her lap.

"Why do you always hide your hands from me?"

"Nobody wants to look at my unmanicured, callused fingers."

It was a side effect from playing guitar. Her fingernails were a little longer on her right hand than her left, and when she didn't put lotion on them, they looked terrible. Especially after recently playing for a long period of time since the indents from the strings remained on the pads of her fingers.

Adam touched a deep scar on the side of his face. "Do you think something like that would bother me?"

She rested her elbows on the table. "I just figured guys liked girls with pretty hands."

"I like your fingers just fine."

She held her middle finger up, an elfin smile on her face. "Do you like this one? It's my favorite."

He grabbed her finger and gave it a playful shake. "Do you ever think about having kids?"

It was an odd change of topic, and she pulled her hand away.

"I just mean the whole thing with Silver and Logan got me to thinking about kids, I guess."

"Do you?"

"I can't."

She arched her brows. "If Logan and Silver bring home a child, they'll have proved you wrong. If you want kids, you can have them. They don't have to come out of your body. I'm undecided. I'm really into my career right now. Maybe someday."

"What if you meet someone who isn't human?" His cheeks mottled with a pale red, and he cleared his throat. "You might meet a Shifter."

"Or a Chitah. Or maybe a Mage," she suggested, letting

the comment hang in the air for a few seconds. "I can't plan my life; all I can do is live in the moment. If I meet someone I can't have children with, then maybe that's the way it's supposed to be. Or maybe we adopt. Or maybe I'll decide I don't really want kids and my life is enough."

"Would your man be enough?"

Sadie leaned forward, her forearms resting on the table. "I don't know, Scratch. I'll give you the scoop when he gets the courage to ask me out."

"Maybe he already has and you turned him down."

She chuckled. "Then he didn't try hard enough. Whoever wants me is going to have to fight for me."

Adam gave her a crooked smile. "They sure as hell are going to have to fight the Cross brothers."

"I wouldn't have it any other way," she said, reflecting on how much she loved her family and their protective nature. She'd never had anyone look out for her like that, and even if it seemed a little overboard, it's what made her adore them that much more.

"You must add a whole new level of stress to their lives."

"Trust me, I know. I can't even get into a car that isn't equipped with airbags."

He rested his chin in the palm of his hand. "So much for taking you out on my bike."

She sat back in her chair, figuring now was as good a time as any to bring up his mode of transportation. "You should buy a car. Motorcycles aren't safe. You could have skidded off the road in this weather and hit your head."

"Are you worried about me, Kitten?"

A little, she thought to herself. Enough that when Adam had called and said he was on his way over, she waited on the first floor, butterflies in her stomach as she watched the snow coming down. Even worse was when he came in and handed her the flowers. Adam wouldn't have bought her something like that, but for a fleeting moment she kind of wished he had.

Sadie stood up and stretched her sore arms. "Why don't you help clean and set the table while I pick up the living room? Then we'll reheat the food when everyone starts to get hungry again."

She crossed the room toward the fireplace, noting that Justus and Page were fast asleep in each other's arms. Those two were perfect together, and she still couldn't get over the painting. Novis was reclined in a chair, eyes hooded and watching the firelight. Sunny had gone upstairs to take a shower and change into her pajamas. Sadie bent down and collected a few bows, ribbons, and torn pieces of wrapping paper that had been missed.

When the puppy let out a small whimper, she turned to look. Simon's pillow had fallen to the floor, and the puppy was standing on his chest and licking his mouth.

Sadie smiled at Ella, who was sitting on the floor beside

him. "What are you going to name him? You better pick something before Simon does."

Ella watched Sadie's lips, probably to make sure she wasn't going to say anything else. "I've never had a puppy before."

"You'll need dog food and a leash," Sadie said. "Tonight you can probably feed her some vegetables. All that turkey will give her gas."

Ella smiled and crossed her ankles. Silver had lent her a pair of sweatpants and a cotton shirt to sleep in. Apparently Ella had forgotten to pack pajamas. "Adam said the puppy's a girl. It figures that a girl would have been following Simon."

"Are you going to keep her?"

"I don't see how I could give her away. She came to us, and just look at all the joy she's brought."

Sadie nodded. "I think you might have just found your name."

Ella glanced up at the puppy and smiled. "Joy. I like that."

When Sadie stood up and searched the room for empty glasses and dishes, something caught her eye. There were now *four* stockings hanging from the fireplace instead of three.

As she approached the mantel, she realized a green one had her name written at the top with a glitter pen. One of her brothers must have done this before they left, even though they had agreed no gifts. Curious, she dipped her hand inside and pulled out a package of guitar strings.

Which was exactly what she needed.

Her brothers would have never bought her these. They didn't know the first thing about music and usually gave her expensive gifts she didn't need, like perfume or jewelry.

Sadie turned around, her gaze traveling across the room. Adam peered over his shoulder with a ghost of a smile before getting up and leaving the room.

CHAPTER 17

Finn and the Cross Brothers

FINN CARVED A SMOOTH ANGLE in the small piece of wood, a chip falling onto his lap.

Levi glared over his shoulder from the driver's seat and growled, "Will you stop whittling that shit all over my truck? I'm going to be finding splinters for weeks."

"I'll clean it up," Finn said. "It calms my nerves... unlike your driving."

Leo pulled down his visor and the light flicked on, allowing Finn to see his perturbed expression. "It doesn't exactly calm *my* nerves to know that if Levi slides off the road, your knife is going into my back."

"Are you saying I'm a bad driver?" Levi fired back. "I could drive this piece of machinery across a frozen lake without fishtailing. Don't challenge my skills."

Finn put away his knife and tucked the block of wood into his small bag. The seats in the back of Levi's truck were a tight fit, and he was beginning to feel like a sardine. Lucian's phone illuminated his face as he used it to track their location.

Finn wrinkled his nose. "Ah, man. Who did that?"

Levi glanced at Leo. "You shouldn't have had that extra helping of turkey."

"Quiet, Levi. Concentrate on the road."

Lucian thumped Finn on the knee. "He who smelt it dealt it."

Leo's window opened, and a blast of frigid air shot in the backseat and blew snowflakes into Finn's hair.

He grabbed his coat from the floor and scowled as he put it over his chest. "If you guys keep this up, a few engine sparks might blow us to smithereens."

Lucian chuckled and leaned forward between the seats. "Look for the turnoff, Levi. You should see it any minute."

Levi gripped the steering wheel and gradually slowed to a stop. "I can't even see my windshield. Leo, get out and scrape."

Leo threw his brother an irritated glare as he grabbed the scraper and got out of the truck to clear the windshield.

Finn patted the back of Leo's seat. "Roll up his window before I freeze to death. I'm not an Arctic wolf."

The window made a crunching sound as it went up.

Levi sighed. "I don't like the looks of this weather. What if they spun off the road?"

Lucian snorted. "Rescue teams wouldn't have any trouble

finding your truck—they'd just follow the heavy fragrance of turkey farts."

"Hey, that time it wasn't me." Levi reached between the seats and found a knit hat and pulled it over his head. "I have a feeling we might be footing it once we get off the highway. What's the maximum distance to the cabin from the turnoff, Lucian?"

"A hair over two miles."

Finn looked out the window and couldn't see where the road ended and the grass began. Chitahs could run exceptionally fast, but not necessarily through snow. The Cross brothers had long legs, however.

"Someone will have to carry the food," Finn pointed out. "We have three coolers and four bags. Plus our personal stuff."

"You're a big guy," Lucian teased. "You can swing it."

Finn wasn't a stranger to manual labor. After all, he'd lived most of his life as a slave. But he was more concerned about them losing their way and getting lost in the woods. He could survive fine by shifting into his wolf, but he wasn't so certain how his brothers-in-law would fare. They were stout men, but the temperature was unforgiving.

Aside from that, he worried for Silver. A bond existed between them, one forged by blood and loyalty. Finn had always felt an unexplainable connection with her. Maybe it had to do with the fact they shared the same DNA or perhaps it was their circumstances in life that drew them together, but he loved her fiercely. She and Logan had taken him under their wing and not only given him a home but a fresh start in life. It wasn't in his alpha nature to sit idly by when her life could be in danger, and the thought of her in trouble made his wolf pace restlessly inside him.

Lucian tossed his phone on the seat. "Signal went out."

The wind whistled outside like a train, and after Leo scraped all the windows around the truck, he got back inside and warmed his hands in front of the vents.

Levi switched on the radio, and the truck rolled along to Stevie Wonder's "Superstition."

"This is bad luck," Lucian grumbled, looking out the window.

Levi tilted his mirror. "Nothing about Stevie is bad luck."

"Let me know how you're feeling about luck if a black panther crosses our path or lightning hits the truck."

That made Finn wonder if there were any Shifters living out here. They often chose rural areas where they could buy up a lot of land for their animals to roam.

The truck skidded.

"Watch it," Leo warned, pointing at a pole.

"I see it, I see it," Levi said, steering left.

The worst thing they could do was drive off the road and end up in a ditch, so they had to pay close attention to the markers since there weren't any clear tracks to follow. Not until they headed down another turnoff and the trees canopied some of the road.

"I see tracks," Levi said. "I bet that's them."

The back end of the truck suddenly fishtailed, and everyone gripped what they could when they hit a hard bump and slid off the road. Finn pushed his hands against the roof, his eyes wide as they came close to rolling over.

"Guess that's it, boys." Levi shut off the engine. "Carry what you can; we walk from here."

Finn hopped out of the truck with his bag slung over his shoulder. Levi and Lucian jumped into the bed of the truck and were looking at some rope and pointing at the handles on the coolers.

"Here, you can use this." Finn handed Lucian his knife so he could split the rope.

Leo put on his gloves and grabbed the sacks. They'd brought everything but weapons. Chitahs were superior hunters and fighters, and they could kill a Mage with one bite. Between the three of them, they had no worries about who they might be up against. Their only concern was bringing the turkey.

Finn searched inside the truck while they gathered up the food. "Where's the flashlight?" he yelled out.

As his brothers gathered behind him, he could hear the snow crunching beneath their boots.

Finn turned around, a white plume of breath accompanying his words. "I can't find any flashlights."

Levi pulled his hat over his ears. "You looked?"

"I already went through everything in the backseat during the ride," Finn said. "Unless you have a secret compartment I don't know about, it's not in the glove compartment, under the seats, in the armrest thing, along the doors—"

"Here, let me look."

Levi leaned inside, ass out, and searched his truck.

The brothers stood watching, freezing pellets tapping against their jackets and hoods.

Levi finally emerged. "We'll be fine without them."

Lucian shoved past him and got inside, tossing stuff out of the glove compartment. "How do you not have a flashlight in your truck? You have a condom, beef jerky, tweezers, deodorant, a Butterfinger…"

Finn smirked. "You could be on *Let's Make a Deal.*"

Lucian hopped out and slammed the door. "Yeah, but he'd lose if Monty asked him for a flashlight."

Finn came to a decision and set down his bag.

"What are you doing?" Leo asked, watching Finn take off his coat.

"Shifting. My wolf can navigate through this snow with no problem, and he can sniff out the cabin and lead the way."

Levi nodded. "Good idea. We'll bring your clothes."

The men trudged down the road, staring into inky darkness with no lights or stars to guide their way. Chitahs could see a little in the dark, so he didn't have any concerns about them not seeing his wolf.

In a fluid movement, Finn shifted. He shook his head and raced ahead of the men, communicating to his wolf what they needed to do. Finn lifted his nose and drew in the scents around him. He could smell fresh ice, wet earth, pine trees, turkey, and in the distance… smoke.

CHAPTER 18
Silver and Logan

LOGAN STOKED THE FIRE, AND it didn't take long for heat to permeate the small cabin. There were only two windows—one by the door and the other over the sink. I'd shaken out all the blankets, but our dilapidated surroundings depressed me. Here we were, on the most important day of our lives, about to make an impression on a child who would soon be ours, and we were surrounded by filth. No food, no running water, no warm bed.

I had removed the thermal pants from beneath my jeans and began searching for something to keep me preoccupied. "Logan, what if this really *is* a trap and they plan to kill us for the money?"

He launched to his feet and his fangs punched out. "Then I'll tear out their throats. Any man who comes after my family will taste his own mortality. Sharpen your light and stay alert."

When I placed my hands on his chest, his canines retracted. Logan gazed down at me, firelight brightening the ends of his blond hair, his brow pensive, his shoulders broad and formidable. Nothing about him frightened me.

But it made me wonder if he would frighten the child. What if this was a teenager who'd had a traumatic experience with Chitahs? The odds were great that this child might be reluctant to accept us in the beginning, but I hoped in time we could shower enough love on him or her that they'd realize it doesn't matter what Breed you are. Love is an emotion that knows no race, gender, or age.

Logan drew in a deep breath and swung his eyes toward the door. "Someone's coming."

I ran past him, wiping the condensation off the window and peering into the darkness. A shadow moved in the distance.

When Logan opened the door, I could see more clearly as light spilled out of the cabin. It looked like a bear approaching on its hind legs. The visitor was wrapped in dark furs, and nothing human was visible except for two legs. Logan stepped onto the porch and waited by the steps. I knew he was using his keen sense of smell to detect deception or danger.

"Are you Logan Cross?" a woman asked, out of breath.

"I am."

"Did you bring the money?"

"It's inside. Come get warm, female."

I backed away from the door and watched as she took off the trapper hat, flecks of snow and ice scattering to the clean floor. She appeared in her forties with dark hair and nothing distinct about her looks except plump cheeks and a small scar on her chin.

Logan shut the door and joined my side. "You didn't bring the child? We had an agreement. I won't give you the money without the child."

"Where's your car?" I asked in a panic. "You didn't leave him in there, did you? The temperature is below freezing!"

Ignoring me, she looked between us and shook her head. "No wonder."

I frowned. "No wonder what?"

"That you bid for a child on the market. The orphanages wouldn't give a mixed couple a child, would they? What are you?"

I narrowed my eyes. "Childless. Does it matter what my Breed is?"

She shrugged. "I suppose not. Where's the money?"

Logan lifted a cloth tool bag near the door and set it down in front of her, unzipping it so she could see the money. He looked up, the black rims of his eyes getting thicker. "Where's the child?"

She'd begun to open her heavy fur coat when suddenly I noticed something against her chest. A cloth sling wrapped around her body, securing a tiny bundle. "I've only got half a bottle of formula left. I hope you brought something."

My heart stopped.

It felt as though I were in a dream when she handed

Logan a bottle and they spoke privately. Or maybe they spoke in perfectly normal voices and I'd gone completely deaf. The entire world simply stopped.

While the woman knelt and went through the money, Logan offered her a glass of water, which she waved away.

I'd taken a few steps back, speechless, unable to think clearly.

This was real.

And not just a child, but a *baby*.

Babies were rare on the black market, so we had always been prepared to receive a small child or even an older one. That had never been an issue with us.

She pulled open the sling and handed the little bundle to Logan, who cradled the infant against his chest, his large hand practically obscuring the baby's head.

"Jiminy," he whispered. Logan stripped his attention away from the child. "And the mother?"

"You won't have to worry about her coming to claim her child. She was forced to give him up, but she accepted this fate." After the woman secured her coat and lifted the bag of money, she took one last look at us before disappearing into the cold, dark night. "Good luck, and may the fates be with you," she called out in the distance.

My feet were cemented in place. Logan shut the door, his eyes sparkling as he looked down at the baby. I'd never seen such a soft look on his face aside from when he looked at me.

After a moment, he centered his eyes on mine. "It's a boy."

With those three words, my baby was born. Tears flooded my eyes, and my knees weakened as I stepped back and collapsed on the couch.

Logan strode forward and knelt in front of me, placing the infant in my lap. The little boy squirmed before yawning and going back to sleep. "His name is Lakota. I think we should keep it to honor his mother. If she was forced to give him up, someone must have hurt her. The Relic said he's a Shifter—probably a wolf, but she can't be certain since she didn't have information on the father. He's ours, Little Raven. This is our son."

I picked Lakota up, making sure to support his head, and placed him against my heart. His skin was so soft, and he sighed as if the warmth of my body soothed him. The pieces of my life were locking together in that moment—a love story that had begun on the day I met Logan and had finally found its ending.

I pressed my lips against his dark, silky hair. "Why would she have sold him on the black market? Why not give him to an orphanage?"

"I didn't ask, Silver. The mother doesn't know his fate, and I didn't want to risk offending the woman or she might have walked away from the deal. I just hope the money we paid her does some good in this world."

Logan leaned forward and drew in a deep breath, owning

Lakota's scent. It was something Chitahs did when they wanted to imprint someone to memory for life. He'd done the same with his younger sister and also with me.

I turned Lakota in my arms so that we could both see his pudgy little face. His skin was darker than mine, his hair a rich brown. "He must be Native American with a name like that. Maybe that's why the mother gave him that name, so there would be no question about his heritage. What a handsome little man."

As if hearing us, the baby opened his eyes. Blue eyes.

I looked down and noticed his newborn diaper. "How old is he?"

"Days."

"We don't have diapers. We don't have food," I said, kicking myself for not having planned for the unexpected.

Logan brushed my hair back, his voice soothing. "I'll cut up a few shirts and make diapers. The bottle might last until morning, and we'll head back early. You have nothing to worry about, Little Raven. I'll protect my son."

I splayed Lakota's tiny fingers, looking closely at his fingernails and memorizing every little detail as if he might disappear.

"He should know that he's adopted," Logan insisted. "I don't want to begin our relationship with a lie."

"I agree. We won't keep secrets from him. But what if the mother finds us? What if she wants him back?" Suddenly my heart clenched, and I was overcome with a protectiveness I'd never known.

"We'll cross that bridge when we come to it, but for now, he's ours."

We quietly watched Lakota for a long time, mesmerized by this precious little life that had fallen into our world like an angel. I suddenly imagined our future. His first words, his first giggle, a little boy learning how to brush his own teeth, trips to the park, teaching him how to tie his shoes, his first girlfriend, and eventually watching him grow into a man. What kind of influence would we have on his life? Would he be a strong leader, a compassionate soul, an attentive husband?

When he began to wriggle and cry, Logan sat beside me and nestled the baby against his chest. Lakota instantly calmed when Logan turned on his motor and began purring.

I got up and wrung my hands. I didn't know the first thing about newborns. I'd been around everyone else's babies, but I couldn't remember how much or how often they ate. What was different about raising a Shifter baby? What if we were snowbound in the morning and trapped here for another few days? I couldn't magically produce milk from my Mage nipples.

"Female, take a seat," Logan barked. "You're burning my nose with all that doubt."

"I can't help it! It's twenty degrees out there and our car is too far up the road to walk with him. He'll freeze!"

Logan chuckled. "I cleared the path, remember? I'll clear

it again. The SUV is not as far out as you remember. We have warm coats."

"But she didn't leave us that baby sling thing! What if I drop him?"

Logan threw back his head and rocked with laughter.

"This isn't funny."

"I do love it when you're riled up."

I cocked my head toward the door, my heart racing.

"What's wrong?" he asked, alarm in his voice.

"I don't know. I thought I heard something outside. Are there bears out here?" When I looked out the window, something large was moving in our direction.

An animal.

CHAPTER 19

The end

LOGAN HANDED ME THE BABY. "Get upstairs and stay low!" His fangs punched out when he saw the animal charging through the snow toward the cabin.

I rushed up the ladder, gripping the baby tight against me. When I reached the loft, I wrapped him in a blanket and then peered over the edge of the loft.

A hollow note hung outside the door—the howl of a lone wolf.

Logan crouched, ready to open the door and spring into action.

"Wait!" I hurried down the ladder. "Let me see." I scrambled to the window and looked closely, having recognized the familiar tone. "That's Finn. I'm positive. Open the door!"

He gave me an apprehensive glance.

"Trust me, I know my brother."

When Logan opened the door, a wolf lunged and knocked

him to the floor. Finn excitedly licked at his face and neck, tail wagging, toenails clicking across the wood.

I began to close the door until I noticed three shadows heading in our direction.

"Who goes there?" I yelled out.

"Santa!" Levi boomed.

I breathed a sigh of relief as Levi, Leo, and Lucian came into view. They were dragging something behind them like the three wise men with their bags of frankincense and myrrh.

Leo reached the porch first and wrapped his arms around me. "Are you safe?"

"We're fine. Everything's fine. Get inside where it's warm. Your nose is redder than Rudolph's."

He lifted his bags and set them inside the door before taking off his boots and heading to the fire.

I gave Lucian a hug, even though he wasn't the most affectionate man. He dragged a cooler in behind him, and it made a racket against the wood floor when it tipped over.

"Shit," he muttered.

As soon as Levi reached the steps, he collapsed on the porch with a dramatic thud. "Sweet Jesus, never again."

I pulled the hat off his head and tossed it inside. "What are you guys doing here? We told you not to come."

He took my hand and stood up. "We're the Cross brothers. That's how we roll. Did you think we were going to let you risk your lives or starve to death out here?"

I stood on my tiptoes and kissed him on the mouth. "I'm thinking that maybe I'm just the luckiest woman who ever lived to have brothers like you."

Levi might have been blushing, but I couldn't tell since his cheeks were already aflame from the cold. "Yeah, my kisses do that to people. Step aside. We brought supplies."

Once the door closed, the cabin was alive with activity. Finn's wolf paced the room, whimpering and behaving peculiarly.

The boys stripped out of their winter gear and stood by the fire to thaw out.

I knelt down and opened a large plastic bag. "Who packed all this?"

Levi was lying flat on his back, puddles of water forming around his wet socks. "The girls. Us. Everyone."

Inside one of the bags was a warm afghan that belonged to Page. There were also a few outfits for children ranging from newborn to age four. She'd also stuffed a few diapers in there, even though they were too large. My heart warmed. They must have been saving things like this just in case.

Another bag had toothpaste, toiletries, and…

I held up the canister of baby formula to show Logan, and he nodded as if to say it was going to be okay.

Leo sat with his back to the fire, his hair almost matching the radiant flames of burnt red and gold. "It's a good thing we arrived here first. I apologize if this goes against the agreement you made, Logan, but we can't have you doing this alone."

Levi eased up on his elbows. "The roads are a mess. I hate to break it to you, but I don't think your contact's going to make it out here. Most of your tracks were buried by snow, and everything's starting to freeze."

It made me wonder how the Relic had managed. She must have either come from the other direction on the road or perhaps walked from a nearby cabin.

When a cry sounded from above, everyone's eyes drifted upward—a bewildered expression on their faces.

Finn's wolf bounded toward the ladder and tried in vain to climb it. When he barked a few times, Logan shoved him aside.

Levi rose to his feet. "Is that what I think it is?"

Logan climbed the ladder and then returned with a small bundle. Lakota didn't have on clothes, only a diaper. He'd probably never worn clothes since he was taken from his mother so quickly.

Logan angled his arm so everyone could see the infant. "Meet your nephew, Lakota Cross."

I stepped forward because I wasn't sure of what I was seeing. There were actually tears in their eyes, and I'd never seen these men so emotional.

"Don't give him to me," Levi said, his voice quavering. "I'll drop him on his head."

I touched his arm. "No you won't. You'll protect him. He's your nephew."

Logan handed the baby to Levi, who held him flat against his chest instead of cradling him in one arm. Levi's large hand splayed across Lakota's back, and he gently swayed his body as if he'd done this a million times.

"I'm your Uncle Levi," he said softly. "I'm going to show you how to be a brave little man."

Leo gripped Logan's shoulder, a proud look in his eyes. "My deepest congratulations, brother. If you don't mind the question, what is he?"

"A Shifter," Logan replied, lifting his chin high. "My son is a Shifter."

After they passed the baby around, I realized Finn wasn't going to sit still until he was introduced.

"Let Finn see him," I said.

Logan shook his head. "He should shift. He might hurt the baby."

"Finn would *never* hurt a baby," I said. "I know that about his wolf. He's dangerous, but he's fiercely protective. You have to trust him."

There wasn't a thread of hesitation on my part. Finn's wolf had comforted me long ago in one of the darkest moments of my life, and I'd come to know him as a man who protected those he loved. I cradled the child in my arms and dropped to my knees.

Finn's wolf approached slowly, his nostrils twitching as he sniffed the baby's feet. His tongue came out and licked Lakota's tiny toes, making him squirm. Then he nestled his head on the baby's belly and closed his eyes. I'd never seen him do anything like that before, and the love was palpable.

Within seconds, Finn shifted to human form.

Tears gathered in his eyes, and he sat before me, gazing down at the small infant. "He's a wolf."

I smiled. "He's your nephew."

"He's my brother."

Brotherhood was a wolf thing—a term that Shifters used among those they loved and shared a bond with as they would a brother. This union couldn't have been planned more perfectly. A child we'd always wanted and a spirit wolf that Finn needed. Now he would be not only an uncle but a mentor, and I had a feeling Lakota would become a strong wolf because of it.

"Uncle Finn needs to put some pants on," Levi said with a chuckle.

Finn stood up and put on a pair of jeans that had been stuffed in a bag near the door. Then he quickly returned and knelt in front of me. "Can I hold him?"

I wanted everyone to hold him, but I suddenly found myself struggling with the feeling of never wanting to let go of my child. I knew I'd have a lifetime with him, so I placed him in Finn's arms and let the men admire their little nephew while I fell into Logan's embrace.

"We brought resources," Lucian announced, opening one of the trunks. "I think Levi shoved an entire turkey in one of these. There's apple pie, vegetables, dressing, beans, and I think Sadie packed the potato salad somewhere in here."

I smiled against Logan's chest, realizing we were going to be all right. We had family, a warm place to stay, food, and donated clothes for our child. I never had a reason to doubt or fear as long as I had Logan by my side. Things would work out no matter what... because we had love.

"He's a beta wolf," Finn informed us. "A strong one."

There are only a few moments in our lives that count—the ones that take our breath away, when our lives change and the world stops turning. Those moments alter our destiny and place us on an uncertain course, but without them, our lives are meaningless.

This was our moment.